THE SECRET
OF CASTLE KILDARE

J.H.H. Milburn

 www.trafford.com

North America & international
toll-free: 1 888 232 4444 (USA & Canada)
fax: 812 355 4082

CHAPTER 1

Twin beams pierced the deep gloom of night. They pitched and heaved as if anchored to the deck of a storm-ravaged ship. They plunged up and down, and swung from side to side, as the car navigated narrow strips of worn, bare earth with grass growing in the center. It was a goat path passing for a road. The manor house lay ahead, silvered by the bright cold of the moon. No lights welcomed us and not a wisp of smoke could be seen from the many chimneys. Shadowed recesses where the manor hid from the light of the moon hinted at dark secrets. I shuddered, suddenly chilled. I snuggled against Mom, and her warmth, love, and closeness made everything right. We would have good times here this summer.

As we drove closer to the manor, a single light came on, illuminating the glass on both sides of the massive front door. It slowly opened to reveal a man and a woman backlit on the verandah. The light behind them shadowed their faces. Maybe I was imagining things, but the way they stood there made me feel like we were intruding. They stepped off the porch to greet us. The woman was in the light; tall, not far shy of six feet, with a bony frame and a plain gray dress. She wore no stockings, her feet in nondescript shoes. No jewelry adorned her body; no rings on her fingers, no makeup to soften her face. It was a hard face, not in the least warm, even though there was a smile as if plastered in place.

Dan Pearce was the man who came to help with the luggage. He didn't smile when Dad introduced himself. Dan hardly talked, just grunted. His bulbous nose was red and huge; a motley array of craters and bumps; dark veins laced his cheeks. The man was a mountain. He stood well over six feet and was heavily built, obviously very strong. His worn twill shirt was open at the neck and the sleeves partly rolled up his forearms revealed muscles large and toned; he was a man used to hard work. Red suspenders wrapped over each shoulder and attached to rough dark woolen pants that he had tucked into boots, the kind sometimes called gumboots in America. Black hair lay unkempt on his head, in contrast to his blue eyes. I thought I caught the briefest whiff of alcohol, but he kept his face averted, so I wasn't sure. While he wasn't totally repulsive, he was ugly and I was happy not to look at him for too long.

Mrs. Greeley, the woman who greeted us with that plastered smile on her face, kept the phony smile as she ushered us into the manor. Her smile didn't make it to her piggy eyes, which were cold and calculating. I smiled back as I shook her hand, my smile mirroring hers as I curled my lips above my teeth in the phoniest smile I could muster. Dad had told us that the two were cousins and shared the cottage behind the manor. Apparently, they had been on the estate as caretakers for ages. Personally, I wished they were not here.

I dismissed the feeling that we were not welcome as quickly as it came. I was too tired to even care. All I wanted was to lie down and go to sleep. It had been a long flight and a long drive through the low treeless, white-sheep-dotted green mountains of Ireland. When Mrs. Greeley showed me my room, I dropped into bed and was asleep before my head hit the pillow.

I awoke very early; I felt cozy and warm. A comforter was on top of me, thick and heavy. It was cool outside my cocoon of warmth, and my nose was cold as I sniffed at the chilled night air. There was silence deeper than I had ever known, so intense that you could almost hear it.

While I was concentrating on the silence, I heard voices in the distance, muted and unintelligible, but increasing in volume as they neared. One was low and the other higher-pitched. I caught only parts of the conversation, however nothing made sense.

"So do ye think . . . will interfere?" said the deep voice.

". . . interfere, but there's always the night," replied the other voice.

"Lord Almighty . . ." said the deep voice.

"Hush about sleep . . ." was the reply, as the voices faded back into the deep silence until I couldn't hear. I didn't know whether I was dreaming or not.

I must have drifted off. When I opened my eyes, daylight had arrived.

I looked at the ceiling and didn't recognize it. Where was I? Was I dreaming? I noticed the walls and they drew a blank. Nothing fit as my eyes slowly roamed the room, desperate for something familiar. Nothing. The ceiling had huge rough-hewn timbers running across it to join with the walls made of large squared rock. It was obvious that they were very thick, since the window from which a shaft of sunlight lit the room was recessed three feet. This place was like a fortress, including the heavy plank door that would have stopped a fast moving freight train.

Then I remembered. I was in Ireland, on the estate that my father had inherited under an ancient law called primogeniture.

Primogeniture meant the first son inherited the entire estate, leaving all of the others out. As a girl, this incensed me, but Dad explained that the law was to keep the large estates intact, instead of being broken into very small plots by continued inheritance. I guess it made sense, somehow. The other children, he told me, inherited in monetary ways. If that law didn't exist, then Dad wouldn't have inherited the estate. Then we wouldn't be in Ireland, so maybe it wasn't so bad after all.

I remembered when we were back at home Dad standing, open-mouthed, as he read the document sent by official mail. It was from the Government of Ireland. It informed him that he was the direct heir to a large estate in that country. He was the last of a line of O'Neills that went back to the original earl. The former earl had died without heirs.

It was time to get up. I shed the warmth of the comforter and braved the chill of the early morning. The call of nature was pressing and there was no bathroom attached to the room. As I put on my shoes, I heard the squeak of the doorknob slowly turning. The door opened a little as I sat there, watching the event unfold. An uninvited head poked through the door and the startled look on Mrs. Greeley's face told me that she was surprised that I was awake. She quickly hid the sour expression on her face with that phony smile.

I remembered the night before. I saw deep cold behind those eyes and detected a sullen resentment.

On a close examination of her face, I could see no merry lines around her mouth and eyes. I think merry lines are a look into the nature of the person. Mrs. Greeley was not a happy woman and tried to disguise her innermost self with an outward appearance of smiles. I knew instantly that she was a woman I would never grow to like.

"Ah, 'tis nice to see that the pretty miss is awake. I trust you had a fine sleep," she said in that falsely sweet voice.

It demanded some sort of answer so I replied, "Yes, thank you." My dislike of insincere people didn't allow me to leave it like that. I have never kept my opinions to myself, as my family will attest. "In America, it is considered polite to knock before entering someone's room." I saw her stiffen in my peripheral vision. I busied myself fussing with the bed and ignored her and the venom that suddenly shot into her eyes.

"When the missy is dressed," she said stiffly, "Take the staircase down the hall. Breakfast is served in the nook off the kitchen."

I smiled back at her, mimicking her mouth-only smile. It was as sickly as I could make it, one that I had practiced in the mirror many times and could use to great effect. I thanked her in the same false sweetness that she had used with me and saw fresh anger enter her eyes. I knew that she knew that I knew she was a pretender and any pretense at nicety was finished between us. We were undeclared enemies and I could have cared less, since I detest two-faced people with a passion. She left in a huff and I finished dressing, the hint of a genuine smile now spreading on my face.

The hall outside my room was wide, long, and bigger than any hall I had ever seen at home, except for public buildings. It ran the length of the manor and I could have laid down over four lengths of my body to span the width. Suits of armor lined either side like iron guardians, spaced at regular intervals, ghosts of knights and warriors long gone. Heavy tables and chairs were scattered here and there, and rugs ran down the middle, covering the old wide-board oaken floors. They were tending to threadbare. Portraits of somber men and women, visages darkened with age, hung on the walls. They were probably old earls and their wives, or horses, or dogs, whichever was the favorite of the moment.

In the middle of the hall was a landing with a staircase that swept both to the upper floor and down to the main floor. From the second floor down to the main floor, the staircase was magnificent as it curved graciously to the entrance foyer—a real showpiece. From the second floor up to the third floor, the magnificence lessened, but it was still grand. This was where the servants slept. On either side of the hall, there were doors that led to other rooms and judging by the number, eight on each side; they must have had large families back then. My growling stomach urged me on. Down I went.

"Hi sleepyhead!" Dad said, planting a kiss on my cheek. I could see that I was the last to make it downstairs. Mom gave me a hug. Everyone was already eating. As I sat down, a young woman entered the room bearing more food for the already laden table. She had a kindly face with a body tending to the comfortable side. A bright smile under thick auburn hair complemented her milky complexion.

"Yer must be Taylor Hall. Why, ye'r even prettier than I was told. Yer may call me Mary Rose, as 'tis me God-given name. I know that we shall be great friends."

I was going to like Mary Rose a lot; I could have listened to the singsong of her lilting Irish accent forever. I learned that she was from the village a few miles away and was hired to cook while we were there.

"And what would Taylor Hall like for brekky?" I loved how she used both of my given names. She rhymed off a great array of choices. I couldn't believe my luck as there was even fish, which I love. Fish was my choice and it arrived cooked to perfection. Mary Rose poured a cup of tea for me. I was astonished. I had never tasted tea before. It was delicious with milk and sugar. In Ireland, everyone drinks tea from an early age. In short order, I became a confirmed tea drinker.

My brothers, Owen and Matt, and my cousin Mike were eating as if this were the last meal they would ever have. They had started with oatmeal followed by fried eggs, ham, bacon, sausages, toast, and home fries. People didn't take breakfast lightly in Ireland.

Matt was lining his plate with a second helping of eggs and bacon, proving once again that he has the biggest appetite in the family. It was almost as though he was hollow and needed to fill up his whole body. Only when he was eating did he stop throwing that small red rubber ball against hard surfaces to catch it. He liked to drive everyone crazy with the constant thock . . . thock sound. Dad had to tell him to stop constantly, since Matt listened infrequently and forgot frequently.

After breakfast, Mrs. Greeley appeared. When no one else was looking, she gave me a hard look from her beady eyes, staring out from her scrunched face. If it was supposed to terrify me, it failed.

"I see the missy found her way down," she said coldly, though no one else seemed to notice. I had an enemy, that's for sure.

"Mrs. Greeley is going to show us around," said Mom, who was smiling, oblivious to the tension between the two of us.

As we walked behind her she led us to the dining room, which was almost as large as our whole house back home. In the center was a mahogany table with intricately carved legs that could have seated thirty people with lots of elbowroom for each. A huge chandelier that held a zillion candles dominated the high, coffered ceiling with several candelabras centered in a row on the table. It seemed very stiff and formal, and I was glad that we ate in the comfortable nook.

Across the main entrance foyer was a sparsely furnished salon that was even larger than the dining room. It was a ballroom for special occasions, a place for receptions and formal events.

Behind the salon was my favorite room of all, the library. It was two stories high, and had a ladder that slid on a rail so the books on the upper shelves were within easy reach. The books on the second floor were accessible by ascending a staircase located at the end of the room. They led to a brass railed balcony that ran around the entire room with even more shelves and leather-bound volumes. There were thousands of them. The whole room had a comfortable dark quiet feel, with an old leather smell from the bound books and deep leather chairs and couches. It drew me in like a sailor to a siren.

"If I'm missing, you'll know where to find me," I announced to all, reveling in my discovery of this absolute treasure.

Mrs. Greeley called the kitchen a scullery. It was large, like the rest of the manor's main floor rooms. It was at the back of the manor. Two huge wood burning stoves were against one rear wall where a chimney was located. I could well imagine how warm the room would have been with both stoves roaring at once. In the middle was a thick wooden butcher-block table, from the sides of which dangled sharp knives and cleavers. Pots and pans hung along the walls and a well-stocked pantry was off to one side. Mary Rose was at the sink washing dishes. All the while, she was smiling and humming a tune, oblivious to our presence, totally at peace.

The second floor, where we had slept, contained bedrooms, two shared bathrooms at either end of the hall, with sitting rooms next to them. The previous Earl had remodeled this floor and installed modern bathrooms. Until then they used chamber pots, and the servants had to empty and clean them every day. That's so disgusting. I wouldn't have wanted to be a servant then, that's for sure.

The third floor was where the servants slept. A narrow staircase led up from the third floor to the attic and ended at a thick wooden door. Mrs. Greeley was about to end the tour, when Mom said, "Let's go up, and see what's up there."

I don't think anyone else noticed, but I saw a crafty look enter Mrs. Greeley's eyes before she answered.

"There's no key," she said, a little too hastily. "There has never been a key, to my knowledge. It was probably lost long ago. As I understand, the top floor is unfinished. There is nothing in there; and it is dangerous, what with exposed nails and all. It is dirty and filled with cobwebs, spiders, rats and other vermin."

That last bit of news ended all adult interest in the upper floor. While I don't like spiders and am not wild about rats, once my curiosity is aroused, nothing stops me. Not even walking into spider webs would stop me. I didn't like the way she seemed to be deliberately steering us away from it and I determined then that I would investigate further, but not right now.

Castle Kildare, the original site of the estate, was visible from the windows of the second floor. It sat in a clearing, a brooding mass of stones that dominated the countryside. The rock walls were dark even in daylight, as if it held within its confines some deep secret that remained hidden over the centuries.

"How old is the castle?" Owen asked Mrs. Greeley, his slender frame taller than her by a few inches. At seventeen, the same age as Mike he is the tallest in the family, two years older than I am; and I am a year older than Matt.

"'tis for certain no one knows," she replied. "It is very old, one of the oldest in all Erin. It was built even before the first Earl of Kildare took possession."

"Why do you call Ireland Erin?" asked Mike.

"'tis the original name that came from the Celts, who were the original inhabitants of Ireland."

"Can we go see it?" asked Mike.

Again, that hint of craftiness was in her eyes as she answered.

"Dear me, no. No one goes in the castle anymore, at least anyone in his or her right mind. Last I heard of going in there, were those that disappeared these many years ago."

Now, I have seen enough movies and TV to know a good actress when I see one, but Mrs. Greeley was a ham. She rolled her eyes and flung her arms in feigned fright as she said this. Still, she did have her audience, for Mom asked what had happened to them.

Mrs. Greeley replied, "'tis for certain no one knows. They just went in and never came out again. The authorities mounted a search, but nothing was ever found, not a trace."

"You mean they didn't find any bodies?" asked Mike.

"Nothing. 'tis a huge place with endless uncharted corridors and countless rooms in which to get lost. A body could get lost forever in the corridors alone. The search party said strange noises came from the depths, evil noises they said, like the laughter of ghosts and demented spirits. It was not a lengthy search. Sometimes on a still night, you can hear them all the way over here. I have heard them myself and can tell you 'tis enough to make the blood run cold."

"Ghosts! That's preposterous," said Dad.

"Now, I know you modern folk from the New World don't place much stock in ghosts or banshees, but this is Erin and things are different here. As sure as I am standing here, that castle is haunted and I'll be the last to set foot in it, that's for sure. As if haunted were not enough, there are the cave-ins that pose a great danger."

"Cave-ins?" asked Mom, rising to the bait.

"Aye. People have died. Buried alive, I'm told. As horrible a death as there is. Some say that the ground is unstable. That's the official view. Me, I know better. The ghosts in that place are an evil murderin' lot. They are the ones behind the cave-ins. That's why no one who goes in ever comes out alive."

Four pairs of eyes met in silent exchange. We would look into matters and determine the situation for ourselves. It was at once both thrilling and scary. Now we were locked together in a silent conspiracy. I tingled with nervous anticipation, for I felt we had passed a point of no return. Our silent bond committed us to a path that would eventually lead to the dreaded castle.

CHAPTER 2

The next few days were ours. We were free to roam the countryside without having Mom and Dad worrying about us. They had gone to Dublin to attend to the problems and paperwork regarding the transfer of the estate. Dad was not happy and kept muttering the word *governments* while he shook his head. He didn't share any of this with us, but told us that he was having troubles with probate, whatever that meant. We were alone with Mrs. Greeley, Dan, and Mary Rose; but Mom and Dad knew we were capable of looking after ourselves and they were so distracted by their problems that there was scant time to worry about us. Since Dublin was almost a day's drive from Kildare, they would have to stay in a hotel. They hoped to be gone no more than a few days but with governments, who knew?

The weather was beautiful, an Irish sun warming the days. Evenings cooled nicely so sleep was easy. There were woods nearby, a forest really, but the locals called them woods. They covered half the estate and well beyond, so they seemed endless. The woods ended near the village, as we discovered on the first afternoon. It was tiny. I doubt that it would even make it onto a map. It was a cluster of stone houses, a church, and a general store that also sold petrol (which is what the Irish call gas) from a single pump. A carved wooden sign hung over the entrance from a yardarm that simply stated "Mick's" in bold letters. Michael O'Reiley was Mick. He was the owner.

It was an old-fashioned store; comfortable with a wood burning pot-bellied stove that drove the chill from the air, since those stone buildings can be cold, even in high summer. The shelves, cupboards, and display cases that rested on the worn wooden floor were stocked with a myriad of goods that ranged from cans of food and meat to hardware and clothes. The place was crammed to the ceiling. A wide assortment of candies caught my eye. Within the glass cabinet were choices from candy bars to an array of loose candy. Sticks of rainbow colors in glass jars were atop the cabinet. I would have to try some.

Mick was small and rotund, with a beaming smile on his open face. His belly amply filled his middle. Stick legs, a small chest, and average head from which sprouted deep red hair completed the man before us.

Matt began to snicker and whispered, "He looks like a walking pear."

The image brought smiles to our faces. Mick was talking with two other men when they noticed us and fell silent.

"Now who would these bairns be?" said one.

"Be ye the new Earl's kin?" asked Mick.

"Yes," answered Mike, "How did you know?"

Mick laughed. "We don't get many strangers around here, even fewer younger ones, since they seem to prefer the large cities with the bright lights. Me daughter's helping at the manor. Her name's Mary Rose."

We smiled.

"So ye be the new Earl's bairns," said the one closest to the fire. "And how goes the manor and old castle? Now there be Americans to take over. Hope ye be rich."

When we had made our purchases and were about to leave, Owen asked, "Are you familiar with the castle?"

"Everyone in these parts knows the castle," answered Mick in a guarded fashion.

"Is it haunted?" asked Mike.

The man by the fire became very serious. "There's some that says it is. Meself, I have not seen any ghosts, but some around here say they have, cool heads among them. Me, I have heard noises and I can tell you that they are not of this world. The sound of them is enough to make your hair stand on end. No way will I be caught dead in that place." He crossed himself as he ended. The other men nodded in solemn agreement. Had we made our decision to explore the castle in haste? Should we reconsider the decision in light of the new information?

The next morning, we explored the woods with mounting excitement and discovered a place we could call our own. It was a small clearing from where we could view both the manor and the castle. This became our secret place where we could be out of the prying eyes of Dan and Mrs. Greeley when they were about, though lately they seemed to be too tired to care much about us. When I mentioned this to the boys, they all agreed that the two seemed much more tired than when we had first arrived.

The castle was even bigger from this view. The walls rose from the ground for fifty feet or more and we could see the main gate with the portcullis lowered in place, as if to keep away enemies that might lurk in the woods. Even in direct sunlight, the walls were dark, as if a sorcerer created the stones in the dark and placed a curse on them before transporting them to this site to be stacked into walls. The top was like the teeth of a large crosscut saw. Open areas were evenly spaced with raised ones, so the defenders could fire arrows from the open area and duck behind the raised area for cover to reload. Open sections were also handy to pour boiling oil on attackers pounding a ramrod at the gates to bust them open. We saw the castle from all sides as we explored. It covered a huge area. We were puzzled about the need for such a large castle in this out-of-the-way place. It was sure easy to see how someone could get lost in there.

Owen was the first to bring up the subject that was foremost on our minds, as we looked at the castle in silent contemplation.

"Do you think the castle is really haunted?" he asked.

"There sure are a lot of people that do," said Mike.

"It seems to me that Mrs. Greeley is trying to keep us away from the castle," Owen added.

"Not to mention the attic. She sure didn't want us to go up there," I said.

"Which brings up the question, why?' said Owen.

"Exactly," said Mike, "When everyone was sleeping, I got up and went to the attic door and found that it was still locked. Funny though, the hinges were freshly oiled and there wasn't a spot of rust on them. Wouldn't they be rusty if they weren't in use after such a long time?"

"Yet there was no key for it, according to Mrs. Greeley. She said no one had been in it within memory. I wonder what's really in there?" said Owen.

We all looked at each other with knowing eyes.

Mike nodded, "It's still being used."

"We should tell Mom and Dad when they come back," I said.

"No," replied Owen, "Let's keep this between us for now. I have a funny feeling about this. We should see for ourselves what's in the attic. Mom and Dad would only slow us down. I'd rather beg forgiveness than ask permission in this case."

"How do we get in the attic?" I asked.

"Maybe we can pick the lock," said Matt.

I don't know what it is about boys, but they seem to dare each other, even though the dare is not always stated. I could see the excitement in their eyes; they were in unspoken agreement to carry out an attic raid. They looked at me to see if I was in, and I knew I couldn't be the lone holdout. I agreed, the last of the conspirators. But honestly, I would have been the first. This was going to be a scary but great adventure.

Nights in the manor were deep and still, almost as if the dark was hugging you. At least that was how I felt when I awoke with my stomach urging me for food. Out of bed I swung, and worked my way down the back stairs that the servants used to get to the scullery. In my bare feet, I was as silent as the night. There were little noises emanating from the scullery that told me the boys were up and doing their best to clean out whatever food supplies were available. This only reminded me of how hungry I was, so I hurried down stairs—cheese, crackers, and milk on my mind.

I was about to enter the scullery when I stopped, for the rustling sounds I heard were different from any I had heard at home. There was no loud whispering. Were the sounds from the boys? If they were, it was not typical of them. I sat on the stairs with a view to the kitchen; I was in the shadows, silent and hidden, but watchful.

My heart almost stopped with fright as a wraith-like creature sped by with a protective arm around something it hugged to its waist. I stifled a scream that was welling in my throat and sat still as a statue, desperately trying to escape notice. Was this a ghost? I rubbed my eyes as if I was seeing something in my mind, but I wasn't. It was real.

I moved deeper into the shadows and waited, while my heart beat rapidly. I didn't understand what this apparition was. Was it dangerous or benign? I would have given all that I had to have my brothers with me for protection. But they were not with me. I was as alone as I have ever been, but I was no longer hungry. Only scared.

My heart banged in my chest like a drum as I watched the dark presence leave the scullery and glide smoothly and noiselessly along the hall. Though I am not a brave person, I peered out cautiously. The wraith left so fast that I had little time to think. Knowing what my brothers would say about my imagination, I followed with trembling knees feeling like rubber, ready to betray me any second by collapsing under me.

The presence went into the library and I waited for it to emerge for a few moments since I knew that there was only one way out of there. It did not come out. The deep of night made it difficult to see. It didn't see or hear me following it, since I was careful to be very silent. While my heart was still thumping, for some reason I wasn't as frightened as I had been when I first saw it. I braved the library by peeking around the entrance as cautiously as I could. I saw nothing. I stepped into the room. Still nothing, so I switched on the light. To my surprise, there was nothing there. Was I dreaming or seeing mirages? My hunger gone, I went back to bed exhausted, nervous and insatiably curious, and excited. There was more to this manor house than met the eye. It would be awhile before sleep overtook me.

I was dreaming of horses, purest of white elegantly muscled, and proportioned, when one of them began to pound on my floor with its hoof. It was calling to me. From a noise that was pleasing, the knock of the hoof became insistent, dragging me from my slumber. I surfaced to a subdued light.

"Are you awake?" Owen asked.

How do you answer that question? No, I'm not awake. No, I'm still asleep. Wait a minute, let me think. What a stupid question!

"No. I'm still asleep," I answered.

"Very funny," he said as he shone his flashlight at me. "Time to get up, lazy-bones. We're going to find out what is going on in this place."

The boys had flashlights. Matt liked to hold it under his face to cast a distorted image while he made strange sounds and faces. But this was not the time for acting the fool and we ignored him.

I remembered the shadowy presence I had seen and was about to tell the boys but decided not to. I thought they would say it was my over-worked imagination. In fact, I was now wondering if I had seen it at all. Perhaps it was nothing more than a very vivid dream, like the ones I had regularly. I suppose that if it was real, then I would have felt more frightened than I did. In retrospect, I was more fascinated than I was frightened, but one is much braver in retrospect.

I was dressed and ready to go. Low wattage candle-like bulbs in thick shades dimly lit the corridors of the second floor. There was barely enough light to show the way to the bathroom. The shadows gave a ghostly look to the portraits that hung on the walls and the suits of armor cast shadows that played along the hallway in the flickering light, encouraged by every jutting corner and every recess. An array of dark nooks and crannies added to the gloom.

We climbed the stairs to the third floor and looked at the final staircase to the attic. I think we all looked at that door with a touch of unease that verged on fear. Who knew what lurked beyond that door? Our daytime courage evaporated while we wondered if there really was such a thing as ghosts. Nighttime does funny things to your imagination. Even the brave front put on by Owen and Mike was running thin, and I really believed that they would have called the whole thing off if either made the suggestion. Of course as male teens, none would admit to fear, even if they were quaking from it. So, on we went.

Old houses have their own noises in the dead of night. Old manor houses are even worse. Every creak and groan jolts the imagination, enough to send shivers down the spine.

Like a patrol deep in enemy territory, we silently crept up the stone staircase that led to the attic. At the door, Owen shone his flashlight on the lock while Mike tried to pick it. He failed, as did Matt.

"I figured the lock would be easy to pick, since this is an old door. I guess they made better locks than I thought," Matt said.

I don't mind admitting that I was very relieved and I thought I could detect a small note of relief in Matt's voice. Hearts pounding, we stood there awhile pondering the problem of how to get into the attic when we heard muted voices from below. They were coming our way and they grew louder as they neared. We couldn't stay on the staircase and let them catch us.

"Quick, follow me," whispered Owen, "Turn off the flashlights." As one, we descended the stairs with the silent swiftness of fear. We tried several doors along the hallway that were close, but none was open. They had us trapped in the hallway, and there was a dim but moving light on the main staircase at the end of the corridor. It was getting brighter as whoever held it drew near.

"Under the table," whispered Mike. We scrambled underneath, breathless in anticipation as we huddled together. With my heart pounding hard enough to shake me, I watched as the lights came upon us. Surely, everyone in the entire manor could hear my heart beating. They were lanterns like the ones used on railways, bulging near the bottom, but backed with a metal dish-like piece so that they could hang on a wall and project light forward. I nearly passed out and I could hear a collective gasp from the boys as the light illuminated the faces. Evil demons were upon us, demons with distorted, near-human, grotesque faces. Were these the banshees? Was the manor haunted?

We were deathly still as the apparitions came upon us, taking no notice as we shrunk as close to the wall as possible and scrunched our bodies to make them as small as we could. The faces transformed as they passed, and we could see that it was Dan and Mrs. Greeley I recalled those voices I had heard on my first night. They were the same. Mrs. Greeley looked directly into my eyes, causing my heart to stand still as I held my breath, but she passed by without comment. Had she seen me? There was no indication that she had. The shadows cast by the lamps played strange tricks. There was purpose to their gait as they made for the staircase leading to the attic.

At the top, Mrs. Greeley reached into her apron pocket and pulled out a huge ring of keys, selected one, and with a quick twist, unlocked the door. They disappeared through the door, which they closed behind them.

"I thought she told us there was no key for the attic and that it was a dangerous place," I said.

"She said she had never been in there," added Owen.

"So why do you suppose she doesn't want anyone in there?" asked Mike.

"What are they doing in there anyway?" asked Matt, bringing us to the crux of the matter. What were they doing in there?

We emerged from our hiding place, curiosity overpowering fear. Owen crept up to the door and tested it to find that they had relocked it. He peered under the door but was unable see anything. The rest of us joined him, put our ears to the door to listen. We heard a pounding sound, as if someone were hammering on something solid. Were they building something in there? What were Dan and Mrs. Greeley up to?

After the excitement of the night, I had a difficult time falling back to sleep, but daylight arrived and with it our determination to solve the mystery of the attic. We watched Mrs. Greeley carefully but if she had seen us last night as we hid under the table, she made no mention of it. Nor was there any hint in her attitude toward us. She looked tired. Later, we passed by where Dan was hard at work. He too seemed very tired, his movements sluggish. He ignored us. There was no suspicion that they knew we saw them last night. We were free to continue our quest to see what lay beyond the attic door.

The biggest task we faced was to get our hands on the key. We had to have the key or we would not be able to open the door. We watched Mrs. Greeley carefully to see if the key ring was ever out of her sight. Still, even if we did get the key, we could hardly just take it. The missing key would cause suspicion and whatever Dan and Mrs. Greeley were doing would stop. We would never get a chance to discover their secret.

Matt came up with a suggestion and we all listened carefully, since he does come up with some creative solutions.

"Why don't we get some wax? If we can grab the key for awhile we can make a copy of it by pressing it into the wax. Then we can make a key. That way no one will know we have one," he said.

Great, now we only needed to get the key without them discovering us. There was only one way. We had to wait until they entered the attic again, then follow them when they emerged to see if the keys ever left her possession. We solved the problem of sleep by taking shifts; the one to discover them would wake the others. The shifts would be two hours each so the one relieved could then get to sleep again. The watch would be from under the table in the hall where we had remained undiscovered the night before.

Dan and Mrs. Greeley were busy people, for at midnight, just when my shift was ending, they climbed the stairs to the attic once again, disappearing behind the door. I awoke Mike who had the next shift and waited with him while the two were busy in the attic. We then woke Owen and Matt, and we all waited for the two to be finished. They were in the attic three hours before we heard the rattle of the key in the lock. They emerged and retreated down the stairs. We followed silently, careful not to bump into anything.

We could hear their conversation as they descended. "Do ye think we're getting closer?" Dan asked.

"Hard to say," she replied. "But it sure don't help havin' the O'Neills and their brats here for the summer. Ah well, if we don't find it now, we'll have the fall to ourselves and time enough then, 'tis hoped."

"Sure hope we find it afore then. I'm getting mighty tired of this."

Mrs. Greeley was the last to speak, "Just you remember, when we find it we can kiss this goodbye forever."

Brats, huh? I was about to give that woman a piece of my mind right then, but managed to hold myself back. It wouldn't do us any good to let them know we were on to them.

They separated, Dan to the back door, Mrs. Greeley to the scullery. The rattle of the keys interrupted the stillness. When she emerged, the keys were not with her. She had left them before following Dan.

We were excited as we went to into the scullery, though that turned quickly to dismay, since the keys were not to be seen anywhere. We looked everywhere, under tables, behind the stoves, in cupboards, even in wood bins. Matt finally found them hanging at the side of the butcher-block table. He held them up in triumph. Great, we had them. Then we realized that there were at least a dozen keys on the ring.

"How do we know which one it is?" asked Owen.

I looked at the keys with a sinking feeling when Mike's face suddenly lit up. "Wait a minute. Didn't she have the keys in her hand?"

"Of course, that's obvious," said Owen. "Why the question?"

"Because the keys are in a ring and the last one she used must be at the end of the ring. At least at one end of the ring, so that narrows the choice to two keys."

I got very excited thinking that Mike was brilliant, when a dark thought crossed my mind. "What if she mixed up the keys?"

Mike shrugged. "Got any better ideas?"

I shook my head.

"I do," said Matt.

"You do what?" asked Owen.

"I have a better idea."

"Really," said Owen with a skeptical look, "And what idea is that?"

"Simple," said Matt. "We take the keys and go to the attic door and see which one fits."

We all looked at one another and burst into laughter. Matt had stated what was all too obvious.

We found the right key using the 'Matt method.' We desperately wanted to go in right away, using Mrs. Greeley's key, but Owen cautioned against it.

"It might be safe, but they could show up at any time and if they found the keys missing, they would know what we are up to. Even if Mrs. Greeley went to the scullery for any reason, she might find the keys missing. I don't think we should go in now."

He had a point.

Mike had some softened wax from a candle he took from the dining room. He placed it on the table and pressed the ancient iron key with the square lock mechanism into it. It was a perfect mold and with the impression in hand, we returned the keys to their place. Mike handed the impression to Matt, who stood there with a puzzled look on his face.

"What do you want me to do with this?" he asked.

"Make a key, of course," answered Mike.

"How?" asked Matt.

"You mean you don't know how? It was your idea," said Mike.

"Oh, no. Now what do we do?" I added.

I could see that Matt was in deep thought. Suddenly he smiled.

"I know. We find some paper and cut the outline of the key so it fits the impression exactly. Then we can find some metal, like a tin can and trace the outline of the key on it. Then we can cut it out with tin snips."

"Pretty thin key," said Mike.

"We can cut more than one and glue them together for strength," Matt added.

"Where can we get a pair of metal cutters?" asked Owen.

"I bet we could get a pair at Mick's."

We went to Mick's to buy tin snips. Even in the wild array of goods, he was immediately able to put his hands on a pair. We then went into the woods, to our secret retreat, where we would complete the job of cutting the key in secret.

CHAPTER 3

We were just approaching our retreat when we heard music. It seemed to be coming from near our secret place. We stopped to listen.

"Who's playing that music?" asked Owen to no one in particular.

"I don't know, but it's very good," I replied.

The music was magical, like the very soul of Ireland, almost a cross between a sea shanty and a dirge, lively yet haunting and captivating.

"Let's go see who's playing it," said Matt.

As we walked toward the source the sound shifted; now coming from our rear, now drifting from in front and then in another direction, and then another. We were walking in circles, trying to pin down the source of the melody.

The music led us deeper and deeper into the woods. We were getting closer to the source yet it remained just beyond us, as if it were deliberately enticing us. In our enthusiasm, we didn't think about getting lost.

"There he is," Matt whispered as he halted and held his hand out for us to stop as well.

We remained hidden in the woods. There was a clearing, in the center of which was a wagon, a bit like a stagecoach but kind of boxy and higher, but without side doors and much more ornate. The driver would sit on a wooden seat where he could direct his horse. Pots and pans hung all around the outside. It sure must have rattled and clanked as the wagon moved. I guess the noise was sort of his advertising. I had heard of these itinerant people who are called tinkers. They not only sell pots and pans, they fix them as well.

This tinker was sitting by an open fire, playing a concertina and humming. It was a glorious tune played by a master. He had his back turned to us, so he did not notice or appear to hear us, since we remained out of sight but watching silently. Over the fire, a metal pot hung from a tripod and a kettle perched on one of the fire-pit rocks had a thin column of steam lazily drifting up from its spout. As we stood downwind, we could smell the aroma from the pot. It was tantalizing and it reminded us of how long it had been since breakfast.

He played for a while before he put his instrument down and without turning around said, "Will ye no join me by the fire?"

Then he turned around and stared directly at us, and we knew he saw us, even though we had stayed hidden. How did he know we were there? Did he have eyes in the back of his head? He had a pleasant face, one that women would have called ruggedly handsome, despite the rearranged features that suggested he had been in an altercation or two. He was tall, and slender, yet well muscled at the same time. He wore a handkerchief over his hair that was knotted at the back, like a pirate.

He coaxed us to him by saying, "'Tis for sure I'm a harmless enough man in need of a chin wag to drive the solitariness from me bones. A lonely life it is that I lead."

We looked at one another, shrugged and went forward.

As we approached, I could see that his pants were baggy, weathered, and worn. They were frayed at the hems, at least where hems would have been. They were short, ending at mid-calf. I half expected to see a cutlass by his side and a brace of crossed pistols in his broad belt with its wide golden buckle.

"Well now, a finer group of young folk would be hard to imagine, that is for sure," he said. A huge dazzling white-toothed grin spread across his face as his deep blue eyes lit up with great good will. His grin was infectious and it caused us to smile back automatically. I suspected that this rogue had more than once kissed the Blarney Stone, as he added, "'Tis the company of young ones that I have been cravin', so full of fresh ideas and imbued with the zest of life. Ye are welcome to share me fire and me fare."

"Who are you?" I asked.

He winked at me and said, "Why, I be Padraic O'Neill. Me friends call me Paddy and since we are goin' to be great friends, ye may as well start by calling me that. And who may ye be?"

"We're O'Neills too. My name is Taylor, and this is my cousin Mike, and my brothers Matt, and Owen."

"Well now, it would seem that we all share a last name, but we can't be related in any way or we would have known of each other. There are a good many O'Neills that dwell in the old sod, and even a few elsewhere to which I have contributed me own fair share, though there's some say me share might have been a tad more than fair, if ye get my drift. I detect an accent I've not heard before. What part of

Erin be ye from?" he said, as he winked again, and his grin spread even wider.

"We're not from Erin. At least we weren't born here. Our family is from here, but a long time ago. We're from America," I replied.

"The Americas? I thought they be Spanish domain."

It was an odd statement, but the moment was lost when Owen quickly said, "It is," and we laughed, while Paddy looked at us with a puzzled expression on his face.

"So are ye here for a piece?"

"We're spending the whole summer here," Matt chimed in.

"Well now, isn't that grand! This calls for a celebration. Tea is near the ready and I have some sweet cakes in the wagon. I'll fetch them right away."

The strangest thing happened then. Paddy disappeared into the wagon and we could hear him rummaging around awhile before he reappeared. I was astounded. I could have sworn that he had two good legs when he went into the wagon, but when he emerged he had a peg leg. I mean a straight, round, wooden peg that ran from his knee to the ground, like Long John Silver from Treasure Island. I was sure he had two good legs before he went into the wagon. I didn't want to mention it as I didn't want to hurt his feelings. He could have been sensitive about it. He changed some of his clothing while he was in there, because on his head was a huge, black, three-cornered hat. A black eye patch completed the pirate appearance. I looked to see if he had tied his leg to his thigh to give the impression of a peg leg, but it seemed natural. There were no strange bulges. I saw by their open-mouthed stares that the boys were just as shocked as I was. None of us said a word.

He had a tray of cakes with him that he placed close to the fire to warm. Then with great dignity, he poured the tea from the pot that resided beside the fire. I don't know if the boys noticed, but he didn't use a cloth to insulate his hand from the pot handle, which must have been burning hot. But there was no outcry from him as he held it. Into each cup, he poured milk from a pitcher and then added two heaping tablespoons of sugar, which he scooped from an old battered tin and stirred. He passed one to each of us and then lifted his.

"I propose a toast," We listened in silence as he intoned his toast. "Here's to happiness and to the fine fellowship of casual friendships formed along the great highway of life, strange as that highway can be at times."

It was an unusual toast, but Paddy was not the usual host to be giving a toast. I took a sip. It was even better than the tea Mary Rose brewed. It was the best beverage I had ever had, bar none. I told Paddy this.

"Why thankee, sweetheart, 'tis only a little honeydew, with a pinch of stardust thrown in for good measure."

He winked his eye again, the twinkle of good humor shining through. I was really taking a shine to this gallant rogue.

"What are you doing here? I mean, why are you here? And what do you do?" asked Matt.

"A question filled with the honesty and forthrightness of the curious young. I like that. I am here to be away from the press of humanity. I find the silence of the woods helps me to express meself through me music. Still and all, I need to fill me belly on occasion, to keep body and soul together, as it is. To do this, I go through the countryside, sellin' me wares and fixin' their pots and pans. The good folks are too far from the stores of mighty towns to attend to their worldly needs. I'm a simple man, in the biblical sense. The wagon is what you might call me store as well as me home. 'Tis a noble callin'," he paused a moment. "And where will ye be stayin' durin' yer summerly sojourn?"

"At Kildare manor."

"The manor is it? And why are ye stayin' at the manor?"

"It's ours now. Our father inherited it." I replied.

"Did he now? Well, he may have inherited more than he knows."

"What do you mean by that?" asked Owen.

"I'm referrin' to the legend."

"What legend?"

"Zounds! The legend of the treasure, of course." He looked at us for a moment as if we were a few bales short of a full load. Then he smiled again.

"But of course ye wouldn't know about that, bein' from the Americas. The legend holds that there be a treasure hiding somewhere in the old castle. 'Tis a vast treasure of doubloons, pieces of eight, silver and gold bars, plate, and priceless gems. 'Tis said the original O'Neill bought his earldom with a pirate's treasure, the main part of which is still intact but hidden all these years."

"Doubloons, pieces of eight? Paddy? What are they?" I asked.

"Money, me love, gorgeous Spanish money. Pieces of eight be pure silver coins that have been stamped hard to make the metal thin so that ye can cut it with a knife or bend them back and forth until they break into eight pieces. One bit is the eighth part of the piece. When something costs two bits, you break off two pieces, or two bits. Doubloons are gold coins of immense value.

"How do you know so much about pirate's treasure?" asked Matt.

"'tis well known in these parts. But O'Neill was not a pirate. He was a privateer. He was a great patriot of England and plunder was the spoils of war, gained in a legal fashion, with the blessing of good queen Bess herself."

"Queen Bess? Who is she?" Matt asked.

Paddy was shocked at this question. His chest swelled and his head reared back in a haughty fashion and his stance was as if he were addressing a class of learning-challenged ignoramuses.

"Odds bodkins, have ye no sense of history, young man? Ye gods, boy, do ye not know that Bess was the best monarch that England ever had? Zounds, there was a woman to fear. Sent her very own lover to the headsman for want of sharing a throne, she did!"

"You almost seem to have known her personally," I said.

"Aye, that I did," he replied nostalgically and then added quickly, "Through history of course. I grew to love her through the centuries. That ancestor of yours sailed as second in command to Drake, if I am not mistaken. Drake was the one who would become one of the greatest seamen that England ever produced. He rose from obscure poverty to become the admiral of all England. He saved England from her gravest danger. Defeated the largest armada ever assembled under Spain or any other country. Those ships were filled with soldiers to invade England and bring her under the yoke of Spain."

"How did he stop the Armada?" asked Owen.

"Fire ships and cannonade. He was a great commander. When the great armada was sighted, and word came to Drake, he was at his bowls."

"He was drinking?" asked Matt.

"Not those bowls," Paddy smiled, "The kind where a ball is thrown at pins. Drake didn't panic in the least. He insisted on finishing the game before he attended to the Spaniards. He judged the wind in his rear strong enough to set fire to some of his ships and send them with a small crew of brave lads into the Spanish fleet that had clustered against the coast of the continent. The maneuver was greatly effective. Deeply damaged the great armada, he did. Then he drove the fleet north against the howls of a raging North Sea. Rather than face Drake again, the armada sailed north to Scotland and then rounded the tip to head south again. They found rum weather along the west coast of Ireland, and gale winds forced many of the surviving ships to founder against our rugged coast. Our fine people didn't take too kindly to the new folk, at least at that time. Many we killed out of hand, but lots survived. Their descendants are those known as the 'black Irish' today."

"Where was I now? Yes. By the rood, a beautiful ship she were; the one your ancestor sailed in. The Pelican they originally named her, a shipshape barque to make any captain proud to command. Drake changed her name in the course of his expedition to the Golden Hind, for political reasons."

Paddy's recital of history had us mesmerized. You'd almost think he was there. He sure looked as if he might have been.

He continued, "During those centuries of Spanish dominion, each year the accumulated treasure would be transported from the New World to the old. It would gather on the Pacific shores to be transported by ship to Panama, across the Isthmus of Panama by heavily guarded mule train to Cartagena. There, the treasure fleet waited to fill their holds with the wealth of the New World. This vast treasure made Spain the richest and most powerful nation in Europe, perhaps the entire world.

"Gloriana, the nickname of good Queen Bess, had a stake in our . . . er, the expedition. Drake, down to one ship, rounded South America by the Straits of Magellan and caught the Spaniard unawares, right on the Pacific shore where he was least expected. He seized a vast treasure in the towns and on the ships with nary the loss of one of our good Devon boys and sailed west where only Magellan's expedition had gone before. Sailed clear around the world he did, the first captain of a ship to do so. As is well known, Magellan died in the Philippines at the hand of the indigenous people before his expedition completed the traverse.

"To Bess, Drake and his men were heroes. She needed money badly as her father, the eighth Henry, had been a spendthrift and there was hardly a farthing left in the treasury. He had hocked the plate and jewels as well. Drake and his men brought a boatload back. 'Tis said no greater treasure was taken before or since. Bess took the largest share as was befittin' for she had blessed the voyage and had invested in it. Her share was enough to finance the entire country for several years, without her having to go to Parliament to beg for funds. Drake and his officers took the next largest share and then the crew. Even the share of the crew made each man set for life.

"Yer ancestor was one of the original officers, second only to Drake himself, and his share was a kings' ransom. He bought the Earldom from Bess, who liked to enlarge her treasury whenever she could, even to sellin' something that really wasn't hers. It cost him a fifth of his treasure. Bein' a careful man, the first Earl achieved the blessing of the local Irish kings, as well, with another chunk of his share of the treasure. A lot of the O'Neill treasure is unaccounted for. Bein' a privateer, the man had a habit of burying his treasure and tellin' no one where it was. All these years, the treasure remains hidden, though 'tis certain many have tried to find it."

You could have heard a pin drop as Paddy told us the story. The silence continued long after he stopped talking. Finally, I broke the silence.

"Why has the treasure never been found? Is it real?"

"Real missy?" he said in a huffy voice. "This is Paddy O'Neill who's talkin', and Paddy always tells the truth. Aye, by God's Legs, it is real."

Wisely, I remained silent as Paddy contemplated awhile and then started talking again,

"Ye know, there is a small poem that's a tad obscure, since few know it; but it is supposed to give veiled directions to the location of the treasure."

"Please tell us," I begged.

"Well, let me see if I can recollect it." He stroked his chin while he went into deep concentration, as if conjuring the poem from some unfathomable depth. We remained silent with great expectation. He visibly brightened with the remembrance of it.

"Commit this to memory," he commanded.

> *When the light of the moon doth fully flow*
> *The eye of the beam will truly show,*
> *When gray to silver hues the rock*
> *The key ye find will strike the lock.*

> *Four eyes are there to light the dark*
> *To point the way, to find the mark,*
> *To reveal the path to the treasure trove*
> *When hand to stone fits like a glove.*
>
> *Look not to the east, nor to the west*
> *Both north and south, directionless,*
> *When at the place of all alone*
> *Hie thee to the bench of stone.*
>
> *Know thee this, ye searchers clear*
> *The treasure's true and very near,*
> *The prize belongs to the pure of heart,*
> *The end is found right at the start.*

"Methinks there is yet another verse but I am not mindful of it just now. I'll dwell on it some. If I remember, I will tell ye. Now, I don't mind sayin' that there have been a few that have tried to make sense o' that lyric, but none have, leastwise not so far. Very rich indeed will be the one who does."

"How do you know all this, Paddy?" asked Mike.

"Well now, young gentleman, ye might say that I have made a study o' some length on the matter. In fact, ye might even say that I am the foremost expert on it."

"Why have you never found the treasure?" Matt asked.

"Well now, young larrikin, I would have no use for the treasure, for I have no desire for the riches of this world. Mayhap it seems strange to you that someone would not want the treasure, but that is the way of Paddy. Me riches are in the good folks who purchase me wares and the friends I meet along the way, like yerselves. Me horse is me friend and me wagon is me home and I have the sky during the day and stars at night and the drum sound that the rain makes when it beats on me wagon or hisses in the forest. I have the light of the bright sky and an endless array of cloud formations that sends the imagination soaring. What treasure can top that?

"Now we've had a fine time together, but there are folks who would worry if ye are late. Since we've had such a grand time and I have taken such a fancy to ye, I have a little gift for ye to remember me by."

With that, he disappeared into the wagon, leaving us wondering what he would have to give us. We heard him rummaging around again before he reappeared. To each of us, he presented a small leather pouch on a long leather thong. The pouches seemed old, since the leather was soft and a deep nut brown.

"These pouches are to go around yer neck, and hang close to yer heart, where it will be out of sight to any eyes but yer own. And this is what yer should place in the pouch, and be most certain not to lose it."

Into each of our hands, he placed a large marble-like stone, the kind they called boulders. They were flat on one side and smooth to the touch, but they were not like any marble I had ever seen. This marble was opaque, a milky sheen as if to mask hidden mysteries. A band of light ran through it, and the band followed the angle of the sun. It was very strange, but beautiful.

"Now these are special and Paddy has been holding them a long time for young ones such as yerselves. Guard them carefully, almost with your very lives, as it were. Tell no one that ye have them. They are much more valuable than they look."

"What are they?" I asked.

"Moonstones, me fancy," he answered, "As mysterious and beautiful a gem as you'll ever find on the face of this earth. The gift will be our secret. No one is to know that ye have them, but if they get accidentally discovered, then tell no one where ye got them, or who ye got them from."

We protested that this was far too great a gift, but Paddy would hear nothing of it.

"Be thinkin' no more about it. Ye be doin' Paddy a great favor by accepting them. Too many possessions weigh a body down, as well I know. Spend yer entire life worryin' about keeping 'em safe.

Afraid someone will steal what belongs to you. Now be off with yer."

"Will we see you again Paddy?" I asked.

"Well now, ye may and ye may not. Life be a strange thing, and our paths may cross again. But if they don't, then we'll always feel warmed by the memory of our grand time together. I shall not forget ye and it is likely that ye will not forget me."

With that, Paddy turned his back on us and went to the wagon to hitch his horse. He climbed onto the high seat and clucked his tongue. Then he lightly tapped the reins on the back of the horse, and waved as he drove off. The wagon twisted and turned as it rattled down the track until it disappeared; Paddy was whistling a chanty that ebbed as he disappeared from sight.

On a whim, we decided to follow him but the track soon petered-out to nothing. It just disappeared. We could find no trace of either Paddy or his wagon. It seemed as if he had just disappeared into thin air.

I smiled inwardly at some of his expressions. I could pretty much guess what *Zounds* meant, but whatever did he mean by *Odds Bodkins*, *By the Rood*, or *God's Legs*? It was a most unusual encounter, to say the least.

CHAPTER 4

"You're late for tea," said Mrs. Greeley in a cold voice as she treated us to her nasty look. "It's cold now, and that's exactly how you'll get it. Maybe in future you'll have the manners to be on time." She left in a huff.

Mary Rose had been standing by, while Mrs. Greeley scolded us before she left.

"Here now, I'll just warm them a tad. What that old battleaxe doesn't know won't hurt her, and none's the wiser. Why, young people have no sense of time. Begorra, you'd think the woman had never been young and fancy free."

There was such a difference between Mary Rose and Mrs. Greeley. The one was so soft and understanding, the other so hard and edgy. Owen took the opportunity to ask a question we were all dying to hear the answer to.

"Mary Rose, do you know of a tinker with a wagon who travels around, named Paddy O'Neill?"

We waited anxiously while she looked strangely at Owen. A small smile played at her lips. Then she began to laugh.

"And who might have put you up to this? Are you having me for daft?"

"What do you mean?" asked Owen.

"So you've heard of the myth."

By this time, Owen had caught on that he should pretend he knew what Mary Rose was talking about.

"What can you tell us about the myth?"

"That he doesn't exist. Paddy O'Neill is a children's story."

"You mean he's not real?" asked Mike.

She thought for a moment as if wondering what to tell us.

"Well, there are those who claim to have seen him, but they have all been children and, as you know, no one takes them seriously."

"Children indeed," said Owen. "Do I qualify as a child?"

"You don't want an answer to that," Mike said laughing, immediately realizing Owen's mistake and trying to cover it up quickly.

"Ah, but I never said that you saw Paddy, did I?" she said as she looked at Owen with calculating eyes.

Owen then realized his own mistake and covered his tracks by mumbling something unintelligible, and then remained silent as Mary Rose continued.

"Now I'm not saying that there is truth to any of the rumors out there, but there are some that say it's the ghost of Padraic O'Neill himself. The original earl died in mysterious circumstances 'tis said. It was very strange, since there was no body found. He just disappeared one day.

"Then there's the legend of the treasure. 'Tis said there's a vast treasure hidden somewhere hereabouts, but I think it's rumor, since there's been many that have looked and no one has found it. Now, finish your meal because your parents are due back at any moment, and you should get presentable for them."

Mom and Dad spoke to us later that night when they had arrived home. "I have to tell you something unpleasant," Dad said as we gathered about him. "Firstly, your mother and I will have to be spending a lot of time in Dublin. We're only here for the night, so we'll tell you what is going on. You have a right to know."

I was worried, since he looked so concerned, and I thought both of them looked tired.

"We are unable to pay the succession duties on the estate."

He stopped when he saw a puzzled expression on our faces. "Succession duties are taxes that the government levies when an estate passes hands. The amount the government wants is so large that we couldn't possibly afford it. This means that the estate will escheat, or revert to the government, since we won't be able to pay. There are issues that still have to be cleared up so we need to go to Dublin again. We have until fall, so we'll enjoy the rest of the summer here before we'll have to leave it behind for good."

Suddenly the comment from the man at Mick's came back to me. Something about hoping we had money. Boy was that depressing. We excused ourselves to regroup upstairs in Owen's room.

"I really hope we don't lose this place." I said

"Me too," said Matt. We all concurred.

"A ghost," Mike said. "Paddy sure didn't look like a ghost to me."

"What did you expect?" replied Owen. "White sheets with eye holes? Any ghosts I have ever read about look like real people because they were real people at one time."

I thought I would be scared seeing a ghost, but if Paddy was a ghost, he sure wasn't scary. Besides,

I agreed with Mike. Paddy did not look like a ghost and, if ghosts were all like Paddy, I had more to fear from people than I did from ghosts.

Then there was the matter of the treasure. Paddy said it was real, Mary Rose said it probably wasn't. Somehow, I believed Paddy. Paddy O'Neill may not have been a ghost, and maybe he wasn't the original earl, but he was real enough and we had proof as I fingered the moonstones about my neck.

"We have to find the treasure and save the estate," I said.

The boys nodded in agreement.

Mom and Dad were back in Dublin when, one night, I heard Owen say, "It's time," as he shook me awake. Groggily I forced myself out of my deep slumber. We had determined to find out what Mrs. Greeley and Dan were up to, which meant that we would have to go through the attic door. We had carefully timed them on several occasions and they had never stayed or gone into the attic this late. Like the boys, I placed pillows under my comforter to make it look like I was still in my room and asleep, in the unlikely event Mrs. Greeley checked in on us. We were all nervous as we began our mission. With mounting excitement, we climbed the third floor stairs that led to the attic. Would the homemade tin can key work?

Owen slid the key from his pocket and placed it in the lock. Carefully he turned the key and we heard the lock clunk as the bolt drew back. He pushed the door open. It worked. We were in. Hearts pounding, we entered. Our flashlights penetrated the gloom while Owen re-locked the door behind us just in case Dan and Mrs. Greeley were to pay a visit, even though we didn't think they would. Owen relocked the door just in case.

I don't know what we expected to find, but this was not it. It was a huge, open, bare room, running the length of the manor, built of the same large stone blocks as the rest of the manor. There were neither the dangerous nails nor the cobwebs so vaunted by Mrs. Greeley. Clearly, that was a ploy to keep us out. But why? There was nothing in here that could cause any excitement. Our probing beams found a staircase in the middle that demanded exploration. It was a very steep set of stairs. We climbed to a room that was much smaller than the lower one. This was the true attic and there were storage trunks scattered about the room with odd pieces of furniture here and there. Another lie told by Mrs. Greeley.

Back down to the main room, our lights revealed that it was in total disarray. At least the inner walls were. Someone was either rebuilding or dismantling the walls, because there were chips strewn about the floor. Large stone blocks were taken from random places in the wall. I poked my head through one of the openings only to discover that this was an inner wall with a small clearance between it and the outer. On a table close to one of the dismantled sections, there was a chisel set with a hammer and a crow bar. Heavy blankets were close by. Was this what Dan and Mrs. Greeley were up to? Then the question was, why? What was the reason for this?

No sooner had we made a cursory inspection of the walls than we heard voices at the door, followed by the rattle of a key being inserted in the lock.

"Quick," said Owen, "Hide upstairs."

We needed no encouragement as we dashed up the stairs and found hiding spots. What were they doing here at this time of night?

We all scrambled behind the trunks, turned off our flashlights, and waited nervously in the dark. We heard the clunk of the lock and anxiously waited while the door swung open. A faint light grew brighter as they entered the room below. Curiosity got the better of me and I craned my neck to see them. Once again, the faces of Dan and Mrs. Greeley showed in a grotesque fashion. I shuddered and scrunched myself as small as I could in my hiding spot. While Mrs. Greeley could be mean and nasty, Dan looked like he could be violent. They paid no attention to the stairs or the upper room where we hid. Of course, they were not looking for anyone to intrude on their solitude. They went straight for the tools and the dismantled section of stones near them. We listened to the rustling below and heard them talk.

"For sure, 'tis becoming a real grind," Dan said as he picked up the hammer and chisel and began to pound at the mortar between the stones. "I'm beginnin' to doubt that there is anything at all, let alone up here."

"Just you remember the coins. We found them up here. Why would there be coins if the treasure be not here?"

Owen leaned close to us and whispered, "They think the treasure's real. Maybe there is something to the legend."

Without another word, they set themselves to their self-appointed task. With the hammer and chisel, Dan began to chip at the mortar that bound the stones together. When he had chipped all around the stone, Mrs. Greeley helped him to pull it from the wall. They pried and levered, grunted and groaned until the stone came free and fell to the floor with a toe-flattening thunk. It was the third in this series, but it was enough for Mrs. Greeley to poke her head in and peer into the cavity.

"Nothing again," she said with disgust.

"They're going to make the wall collapse," I said, a little too loud.

"What was that?" asked Dan.

"What was what?" Mrs. Greeley replied.

"That sound. It sounded like someone talking."

We held our breath while Mrs. Greeley peered into the gloom and remained listening silently.

"I don't hear anything," she replied. Likely the wind. Yer ears ain't what they used to be. Let's get on with it. The sooner we find the treasure, the sooner we can be gone from this God-forsaken place."

They worked for another two hours, each stone taking an hour to remove. Dan was exhausted by the time they decided it was enough for the night. We watched them leave. We listened as they unlocked and then re-locked the door. Their footfalls fading on the stairs told us that they were descending. We remained hidden for a few minutes before Mike went to the door and put his ear to it.

"All clear, I think," he whispered loudly as he shone his light and we all went over. The addition of *I think* was not comforting.

Cautiously, we waited half an hour before we decided it was safe to return to our rooms. Our nervousness had slowly ebbed while we had watched the pair at work, but we were still a little apprehensive. Perhaps they were lurking nearby, ready to pounce on us. Owen placed the key in the lock and turned it. He looked puzzled when nothing happened. There was no click of the bolt retreating. He tried it several times but the key just bent back and forth. The thin metal had become limp from use; it wasn't strong enough to move the bolt a third time. It bent easily. We now had a useless piece of metal with no way of getting out of the attic. We all looked at each other. What now?

"Let's look around," said Mike.

"We're in deep doo-doo," said Matt, mirroring what we all felt.

We all began to search for another way out.

"I wish we had something to eat. Maybe a plate of roast beef and some of those Yorkshire puddings filled with gravy and lots of mashed potatoes and for dessert . . ."

"Quiet, Matt. We don't need to be reminded how hungry we are," I said, cutting off his daydream.

We searched both rooms. Matt and Owen took the upper room, Mike and I took the main. We looked for any openings other than the occasional window that afforded a steep drop to a sure death. After an hour of searching Mike and I gave up. We went upstairs to see if the other two were doing any better. Owen was shaking his head to indicate no luck, when we heard Matt call out, "Hey Owen. Come and have a look at this."

He had crouched down and was staring at the floor. We came over to see what he was looking at. We heard Matt whistle as he stood, shining his flashlight on the floor. Obviously, he had found something. When we joined Matt at the place he was pointing to, we saw set into the floor a square piece of wood with metal ring attached to it. It was obvious that no one had used it in a very long time, since the indentation holding the ring had filled with the dirt of ages. Mike ran his fingers around the outline of the wood.

"It looks like it might be a trap door." He said.

"Let's open it," said Owen.

We took turns trying to pull the door up, but it wouldn't budge. Matt ran his jackknife around the edges to try to loosen the door, then we pulled on the ring all together, but nothing happened.

"There's a crowbar back where Dan was working," said Mike. "I'll get it."

When Mike returned, he placed the crowbar under the ring and pulled hard. Still the trap door refused to move.

"Give me a hand." Mike said.

"A hand you shall have," said Matt as he started to clap his hands.

"Not that kind," said Mike, visibly annoyed.

We all got our hands on it and pulled mightily.

We were greatly encouraged when the trap door budged slightly with a horrific squeal of hinges. It must have been rusted shut for many a year. But it didn't give way completely. We tried again. We were making no headway despite our mighty heaves. We repositioned the crowbar and all heaved on it together. Suddenly it moved again. And then again, as it cleared the floor. Now we were able to open it fully. A black square hole gaped before us. We shone a flashlight into the inky depths.

There were stairs. Narrow stairs. They circled downwards at a very steep angle. We had no idea where they led, but we needed to get out of our prison.

"Let's go," said Owen and he was the first to place his foot on a step. I was next, then Mike and Matt who was not happy to be last.

"How come I have to be last?" he protested.

"Because you're the youngest," replied Owen.

This seemed to settle the matter except for Matt muttering, "But . . . but . . . but."

Owen's flashlight illuminated the descending stairs.

"Watch your step. These stairs are treacherously steep."

That was an understatement. They were so steep that we had to keep our hands touching the cold stone on either side of the staircase for balance.

Down we went, circling again and again. I knew only one thing. We were well below the level of the third floor, but there was no way of estimating how far down we had descended.

Matt suddenly yelped.

"What's wrong?" I asked.

"This stupid rock bumped my head," he replied in his funny way of putting things in his own perspective. As if the rock had jumped out and bumped him. Owen shone his flashlight back at Matt and we could all see the jutting section of the wall that had hit him, or, more specifically, that he had hit. We had missed it because we were hugging the inside of the wall while Matt, different as always, clung to the outside. He probably did this just to be opposite. The jutting stone looked very out of place, especially since the rest of the stones were flat and smooth. It made us curious enough to go back and see why.

Mike felt all around the stone. "I don't think it's attached to the wall. There is a space between it and the mortar." He pushed on it and felt it give. He pushed more. It moved until it was even with the wall. As it moved inward, there was a barely audible click, followed by a large section of the wall that moved inward as if on a pivot. We stood there in shocked silence flashlights revealing a vaguely familiar room. Where were we?

With great care we stepped into the room and shone our lights. Walls of books greeted us. We were in the library. A section of the bookcase, complete with books, had swung open. It was a secret door to a secret staircase. We had escaped our prison and no one had detected us. Better, we now had a way to get back to the attic to check on the progress of the two treasure-hunters; that is, if we could find a way to open the secret door. We left the door open while we searched all around it for a way to reopen it.

That's when we heard voices and saw a light in the hall. As it brightened, we could hear the footsteps. Owen quickly closed the secret door. The lights and voices had to belong to Mrs. Greeley and Dan.

"Get behind the door. If they only see me they might not be suspicious," I said to the boys.

They hurried to hide behind the main library door that always remained open. There were mere seconds to spare before the two appeared. I just managed to busy myself with a flashlight, peering at the titles on a shelf, across the room from the entrance where the boys were hiding. In my peripheral vision I noticed Mrs. Greeley watching me.

When she spoke, I feigned at being startled.

"What are you doing here at this time of night?" she asked eyes cold and calculating.

I decided to take the offensive, since I have heard that it is the best defense.

"That's entirely none of your business."

The shot found its mark and she took a menacing step toward me. She really frightened me, but I held my ground.

In my haughtiest voice I continued, "In case you've forgotten, this place belongs to us, and I will do exactly as I wish, which includes getting a book to read anytime I can't sleep. I wish you a good night," I said with an appropriately noble and condescending nod, as if she were a lowly servant being dismissed. With that, I again busied myself with the books, turning my back on her, really wondering if she would just kill me right then.

"Well, I'd be careful if I were you missy," she sputtered, the wind now out of her sails. "There's no telling what might befall you in the night."

I didn't answer her as I continued to browse the books, pretending to be nonchalant, but barely able to contain the nervous shake of my hands and knees. I decided it was best to let her have the last word and stifle any parting shot that was stalking my fertile mind.

She harrumphed as she left the library. While I had not helped my cause with her, the boys remained hidden. I breathed a sigh of relief as we returned to our bedrooms.

CHAPTER 5

The next morning, I suffered through Mrs. Greeley's mumbling about kids who didn't know their place, and wandered in the night. I listened to her rattle on, and finally had enough. Owen sensed that I was about to explode, and placed his finger to his lips as a sign of silence. Sometimes it is right to remain silent, and now was such a time. But it was too late, I couldn't help myself.

"Mrs. Greeley," I said in a loud voice. "If you have any complaints, please voice them immediately and I will take them up with my parents when they get back from Dublin. They tend to encourage my reading, and would not be delighted to see it curtailed. Otherwise, please keep your comments to yourself."

I must admit that it felt good, but I was definitely not winning any points with her. She left in a huff, a scowl on her pinched face. Owen cautioned me to go easy in the future.

Since she stomped out to the cottage, we took the opportunity to go into the library to look for the secret door. We knew the area where the panel was located. If we could find out how to work the door, we could go into the attic any time we wanted, without having to resort to using either the main door or a make another key.

An hour of poking about revealed nothing. The secret staircase led not only up to the attic, but also led further down; that was intriguing. It was then that I remembered the specter I had seen the other night. It had disappeared into the library. Could it have left through the secret door? Would we be going into danger we knew nothing about if we found a way to open the secret door?

As we were trying to find the way to open the entrance to the stairway, Mike said. "Paddy told us that the poem was the key to the treasure. Let's see if we can remember it. As I recall, the first lines are:

> *When the full of the moon doth greatly flow*
> *The square that's true will fully show.*

Got any ideas?"

"The full of the moon obviously refers to a full moon," I stated, now examining book titles, having become bored with looking for a way to the secret passage.

"Maybe," said Owen. "But it could also mean the time of the evening that moon is brightest."

Trust Owen to find a fault in our reasoning.

"I think there are too many possibilities," said Matt.

"Matt is right. But we have to start somewhere," Mike said. "My vote is for the most obvious, which is the full moon. Somehow, that seems special where buried treasure is concerned. The treasure's been buried a long time. Many have searched for it without success. The full moon won't show every month through the clouds. So maybe there are only a few times a year that it does. What do you think?"

"We'd better find out when the next full moon is." said Matt.

"They have it in the paper. That's simple enough," said Owen. "But the next line refers to a square that's true. What do you think is meant by that?"

"We opened the door to the library by a square stone," said Mike. "Do you suppose that's what it meant?"

"All questions, no answers," muttered Matt.

We thought about it and felt that it was a definite possibility.

I recalled the next two lines.

When gray to silver hues the rock
The key ye find will strike the lock.

"I think the hue of the rock refers to the color of the stone under the moonlight," I said. "But I can't make any sense out of the key striking the lock"

Owen proved that he could upset any theory by replying, "Maybe we are using the wrong context of hue and the real word is hewing, or cutting the rock."

"Just like Dan and Mrs. Greeley are doing," said Mike.

We all looked at each other with questioning eyes.

Too many possibilities, I thought, as I spied an interesting volume about ancient Greek myths. It had been one of my favorite classes in school and this leather-bound volume was thick, which made it irresistible for me. I reached up for it and tried to ease it from the shelf, but it seemed to stick. That was odd. I pulled harder on the book, but it still didn't give. Finally, I gave it a really hard yank but the book remained in place. Then, I heard a click. Slowly, the shelf moved until the passage to the staircase stood revealed. We sat in open-mouthed wonder, until Owen had the presence of mind to close it.

"Just in case the enemy happens by," he said, "It wouldn't do for them to discover this. Let's wait until late tonight and come back to see where this leads."

We were excited and nervous when we met in the deep night to creep down to the library. We wanted to find the treasure before Mrs. Greeley and Dan did. I shone my flashlight on the appropriate book and pulled hard on it and the secret door again swung open. We entered the passageway. We pulled at the stone that hit Matt, and the door closed. This time we were going down, since we wanted to see where the other end of the stairs led. Ahead was a deep gloom that matched the black edge of our fear. If I was alone, there is no way I would be doing this.

We descended the stairs for what seemed a very long time, but then each step was into the unknown and we were very cautious and very nervous and very slow. Fear does have a way of distorting time.

At the end of the stairs, a heavy wooden door blocked our way. We lightly pounded on it to test it and the thuds told us that it was massive and heavy. We trained a light on the surrounding wall to discover that there was a slight indentation beside where a latch used to be.

"It looks like the shape of a hand," said Mike.

"Isn't there a part in Paddy's poem about that," I said. "Let's see if I can remember. It was something like the hand fitting like a glove. Put your hand on it, Matt."

Matt pressed his hand to the spot.

"It feels rubbery but it fits like a glove," he said as the door suddenly swung open and he lost his balance. He was teetering when we reached out to grab him, preventing him from falling. Standing there, our flashlights pointing downwards, their beams swallowed in the gloom. It was as if a doorway to a huge tomb had opened and was about to close in on us. A chill came upon me.

We pointed our flashlights down and the light revealed the stairs. They were narrow and hugged the wall directly below us as they switched back and forth, descending at a steep angle. There was a landing directly ahead of the door and we cautiously stepped out onto it. None of us moved, since the lights showed clearly how dangerous the descent would be when we attempted it.

"Hold the door, Matt," said Owen as he went to the edge of the stairs. But Matt had already moved onto the landing and his desperate lunge for the closing door was too late. A click announced that the door had locked behind us.

"Oops," said Matt when Owen gave him an exasperated look.

"We'd better see if we can open this thing again," Owen said, shining his light on either side of the door. We couldn't find anything, even though we ran our hands all over it, and all over on each side of it. We were stuck. There was only one way to go.

"I guess we go down," said Mike.

"You first, Matt," Owen added, a touch of annoyance still in his voice.

"I thought the youngest went last," protested Matt.

"They only go last when they hold doors open so that we don't get trapped. When they don't, they lead the way into the unknown."

"Oh, joy of joys," Matt replied.

There was no choice. We all knew it was dangerous. Our flashlights could illuminate for fifty feet or so, but they didn't reach the bottom. All we saw were stairs, which zigzagged back and forth as they hugged the wall directly beneath us, and were open to a precipitous drop on the other. There were no guardrails, no handrails. With hearts in our mouths, we clung to each other. Each of us had a hand on the shoulder of the one in front, and we hugged the cold and clammy wall to protect ourselves from falling. We inched down, remaining in close proximity for safety.

Down, down we went, deep under the earth. I could feel the dank air as it clung to my body. I smelled its staleness as soon as the door was opened.

As we descended, the staleness seemed to increase. Every time the stairs switched back, there was a landing, and we took every opportunity to sit and rest, for we expended so much energy out of fear, we were overcome with exhaustion.

It seemed an eternity, but it was probably only a few minutes of sheer terror. Finally, we were down, with great relief.

"Where are we?" asked Matt as he shone his flashlight into the deep inkiness ahead of him. When we aimed the beams of our flashlights ahead, they revealed that we were in a tunnel. We looked at each other. The tunnel must lead somewhere. Where it led, we would find out. Since we couldn't go back, we had to go forward.

The tunnel seemed to go on and on. Our initial jitters turned slowly to concern as it dawned on us that we were travelling a long way from our starting point. In addition, we didn't know where it would end, nor in what direction we were headed, or how to get back. The stone floor was slippery with the constant damp, likely a result of being underground in Irish soil.

Matt mentioned that Mrs. Greeley had talked about cave-ins in this area. Trust Matt. Now I had visions of entombment, which didn't help my state of mind. As well as to where the tunnel led, the other question was, why was it here?

We must have walked for half an hour before we saw the end, a large wooden door. We approached it cautiously, wondering if we would be able to open it. There was no way we could break it down or kick it in.

It was unlocked, which we could see as we approached. There was a latch but no keyhole for a lock. Mike lifted the latch and pushed his body hard at the massive door, to find that it moved easily, and silently. This surprised Mike, as he went crashing onto the floor.

"Take it easy, you're back in civilization now, Tarzan," said Matt, laughing.

"Wait a minute," I said. "I hear something. Kill the lights."

We immediately stood still and silently strained our ears to hear the sound. At first, I could hear nothing. Then it came. It was muted at first, but the noise became clearer and louder as it came fast upon us. It started as a continuous scratching noise, but as it neared, I could hear the unmistakable sound of hundreds of claws on the stone floor. I couldn't help it. I switched on my flashlight and froze for a moment before I screamed. "Rats," I just couldn't help myself, and I screamed again. There must have been hundreds of them. They were huge, some as big as alley cats. I could hear the collective intake of breath from the boys. We screamed loudly in unison, partially to frighten them away, but mostly out of fear. But we didn't scare them. They only slowed, and that was to stalk us. They looked hungry, thin, and evil. They were trying to circle us, figuring out how to attack.

We madly swung our lights and prepared to use our flashlights as weapons. In the light, we could see their beady eyes, naked tails, and long wicked yellow teeth. The hair on the back of my neck stood on end. As we swung our flashlights at the bolder ones who probed our defenses, I noticed that they shied from the intensity of the light.

"Let's get out of here while the getting's good," Mike shouted as he swung his light about the room and discovered the only other door.

"Let's go now," Owen shouted,

"Oh my, yes," agreed Matt. We raced for the other door as the rats chased us. They surrounded us while Mike and Owen struggled with the door. Matt and I swung our flashlights at the rats, hitting a few as they became used to the lights and grew bolder. Our defense would not work for long.

They got the door open and we all ran through as fast as our legs could propel us. Matt was the last through and we quickly closed the door, keeping all but a few of the rats on the other side of the door. We caught a few in the door. They were squeezed to death. The few that made it through lost their courage when they discovered that their comrades were no longer with them. They melted into the gloom, snapping at us on the way.

"Better check for holes," Matt said. "Make sure the rest can't get in here."

Thankfully, there were none.

Our lights showed that we were now in a large anteroom. There were stone benches on the sides and yet another massive door led beyond that. We were now in the mood to get quickly beyond it and leave the rats as far behind as possible. This door wouldn't move as readily as the previous one. It had not been used as often as the one before. It took all of us pushing as hard as we could before it budged. It creaked frightfully as it gave way, as if to declare loudly to whatever lurked beyond that there were intruders. By the looks of the deep dark stone walls, we were now in the castle.

We waited silently, ears tuned for the sound of anything that might have heard us, but there appeared to be nothing. No one came to challenge our presence and nothing stirred to announce itself. In front of us was a corridor. It was wide and long. The iron doors at the end told us that we had found the dungeon. A look through the lattice openings revealed the primitive instruments of torture, and I shuddered to think of human beings locked down here, away from the light. I wondered what deprivations and frightful wrongs happened to them. Many would have spent their last days in this hell, and many others would have wasted precious years of their lives in these sunless, hopeless depths. How many souls had withered and died here? I hoped that my ancestors didn't use it.

Our fascination with the dungeon ended quickly, since we all wanted to be well past it. Another massive door faced us, but again we managed to open it to find that we were in a corridor. But this time, there was a staircase at the end of it. We needed to avoid the rats at all costs We were nervous of what lay ahead and scared of what lay behind. Maybe there was nothing to the stories of missing people and cave-ins, as we were told. Then again, maybe there was. The latter took hold in my mind as my imagination went wild in the dark. We silently climbed the steep stone steps.

It was a long climb and going up seemed almost worse than going down, because I knew with each step that we were going higher and into the unknown. Besides, going up stairs is much more difficult than going down in a physical sense. It's just more tiring. However, we were leaving this subterranean world, and I felt that was a blessing, at least regarding the rats.

I don't know if the stairs we were going up were longer than the ones we had come down on by the side of the manor when we began our descent to the tunnel, but the climb seemed never-ending and our thighs ached with the constant effort. We rested many times before we arrived at the final landing and entered a hallway, where we collapsed onto the floor in utter exhaustion.

It was while we were trying to catch our breath that we first heard the noise. At first, I thought it was the wind, since it started as a low moan. But that increased, and it sounded as if someone was hurt. It was almost a groan caused by great pain, reluctantly released. We were frozen in silence, listening. Was this the ghost?

"What's that?" whispered Matt.

Wide-eyed, we looked at each other with the same question that remained unspoken. What in heaven's name was that?

The moans increased and began to echo throughout the hall so that you couldn't tell from which direction they came. As they rose, the intensity of the groans became greater. It was as if someone was being tortured in some terrible fashion, for the moans swiftly became shrieks. These were no ordinary shrieks, but those of the demented. Above those awful sounds, as if superimposed over them, was the sound of an evil laugh. The torturer. It was like the sound of someone who enjoyed hurting people. I heard a cackle that caused my blood to run cold.

"Let's get out of here," Matt whispered hoarsely.

Instantly we revived as never before. We fled down the hallway with fear-filled feet, the demented laugh, and screams urging us on.

We ran down one hall and up another. We ran into dead ends, retraced our steps until we were thoroughly turned around, and hopelessly lost. It seemed that no matter where we turned, those sounds followed us getting ever closer. We were fleeing for our very lives.

Owen stopped and held out his arms for us to stop as he said, "Listen."

He heard something we hadn't. We stopped and listened as best we could with pounding hearts and heaving chests. Our hearts nearly stopped as we heard the rhythmic slap of bare feet on stone. It was the sound of something heavy running. Someone or something was after us and it wasn't far away.

Fear is contagious. I started to scream and we all began to run as if the very devil was after us. We ran; legs pumping, lungs bursting and breathless, ignoring pain. Desperately we searched for a way out. Even back toward the rats was better than this menace. But the evil was between us and the way we had come in. There was no escape that way.

We ran through more halls and open rooms in a desperate search for elusive escape. Finally, in one of the rooms, we found a window-like opening with iron bars. Fortunately, the dawn was back-lighting it. One of the bars was missing. We squeezed through faster than we ever thought possible, with the help of some pushing and some pulling. The forest was at hand, and we ran as fast as we could until the castle was a shadowy sentinel behind us.

Exhausted we tumbled onto the forest floor.

CHAPTER 6

I didn't mean to scream, but what we had just been through put me on edge, to say the least. The sudden sound of his voice made me jump out of my skin.

"Begorra, if it isn't me young friends from the Americas. 'tis sure I didn't mean to scare ye, pretty miss. Now then, have you been farin' well on the Emerald Isle since I saw yer last?"

There he was, larger than life, as we first saw him looking like a pirate with his peg leg and huge golden earrings, eye patch and large tri-cornered hat. Where he came from, I'll never know. It was as if he had just materialized out of thin air. Strange as it seemed, we had run to the very place where we had first seen him. Was it pure coincidence, or did all paths lead to

Paddy's clearing? Perhaps the safety of this place had inexorably drawn us here.

"Paddy, we thought we'd never see you again," Matt said.

"And why would ye ever be thinkin' that, young larrikin?"

No one spoke until I broke the silence.

"We were told that you were a ghost."

Paddy looked pensive for a while and then laughed loudly.

"'tis a ghost I am, is it? Well I reckon I can understand you thinkin' that, considering me eccentric style o' dress. But come here, pretty miss, and touch me arm. That'll show that I be real enough."

His deep blue eyes willed me forward until I reached my hand out and felt his arm. His flesh was as warm and real as ours.

"Now, does that feel like the flesh of a ghost to you?"

I shook my head.

At this point Owen interjected. "Paddy, how come we never saw the wheel ruts from your wagon? We tried to see where you went and couldn't find them."

Paddy looked at Owen with a calculating eye.

"Ah then, me bucko, sometimes yer eyes do play tricks on ye, as well I know. And sometimes yer imagination can run a tad on the wild side. There is a sayin' in the Fair Isle that'd sum up the situation nicely. *Believe none of what ye hear and half of what ye see.* Now then, who is accusing me of being a ghost?"

"It was Mary Rose, but Mrs. Greeley . . . ," I started to speak.

"Ah, well do I know who that one is and what that one is. Mrs. Greedy is a better name for her. And her man Dan seems to be a shilling or two short of a pound, if'n yer know what I mean. Ye'd best ignore that source of information and best not to mention our meetin' to anyone, but especially her. Now, how goes the treasure hunt?"

"Not well," answered Mike.

We recounted the attic episodes with the searching of Mrs. Greeley and Dan. We told him of the secret passage, and the underground passage to the castle. And about how we found that the castle was haunted.

"Paddy, do you think the treasure is in the manor? Mrs. Greedy, I mean, Mrs. Greeley, thinks it is."

"Well now, me pretty, it appears that she may have found a stray doubloon or two to give great encouragement to that notion."

He winked at me hugely, as if to convey a great secret. It made me laugh and suspect that I might know who put those doubloons there. But if Paddy was a ghost, he was a ghost with a sense of humor and mischief.

"Now about this haunting you found in the castle. If I were a wagerin' man, I'd wager heavily on the possibility that this Greeley woman is behind it somehow. It might bear investigating into. So ye found the secret passage, did ye? I had a feelin' that you were the right ones. Do yer still have the moonstones?"

We showed them to him.

Suddenly Mike spoke up. "Paddy, are the eyes in the poem the moonstones?"

Paddy's eyes lit up. "A brilliant deduction, me bucko. You are as correct as can be. Now you understand why ye must guard them carefully, never lose them, and never reveal their presence. Mrs. Greedy and Dan can smash that attic apart till hell freezes over and she'll never find the treasure, since it's not there."

I looked at him suddenly and said. "How do you know the treasure isn't there?"

Paddy paused for a moment, caught off guard. He stalled by clearing his throat. "Well now, that's a subject I do have some experience on . . ."

He stopped to scratch his head in a puzzled fashion since he seemed at a loss for words. I could almost see his mind racing as he searched for the right ones. Finally, he began to speak. "I . . . uh . . . have examined the poem on many an occasion. I have concluded that the treasure is not in the manor. I cannot tell ye why I know that. Ye must simply take me word for it."

"Do you know where the treasure is hidden?" asked Owen.

Paddy was pensive for a moment. "In a manner of speakin' I do, and in a manner of speakin' I don't, for there are a great many ways to count treasure. Now I know this may be confusin' but the question is not one that is easy to answer. I have taken a life-long interest in the treasure, so to speak. And if I may say so, it has been as much a study of human nature as it has been a treasure hunt."

Matt piped up. "In a manner of speakin' Paddy, why can't you tell us where the treasure is located?"

Paddy looked at Matt, a slow smile playing on his lips. "Are ye mockin' me manner of speech, young larrikin?"

As usual, Matt played the complete innocent. "Who, me?" he asked with wide-open eyes protesting in innocence and a smile on his lips, which made us all laugh, including Paddy.

Paddy then became serious. "Much as I would dearly love to tell ye exactly where the treasure is, alas I cannot. But I can assure ye that it is real and waiting to be found by those deservin' of it."

"But you helped us already with the poem," I stated.

"'tis true, me princess, 'tis true. But Paddy can only give ye general directions, since I cannot tell ye the location. That ye must discover for yourselves. 'Tis certain that the Greedy woman is not deservin' of the treasure, nor is that lout Dan, who be strong of back and weak of mind. But best ye watch those two, lest they get the better of ye. She be a wily one and the more dangerous for that.

"I don't mean to raise alarums, but 'tis a fact that she has an evil bent of mind. I don't think she'd let anything stop her. She wouldn't care a whit who she had to hurt to get at that treasure. Best beware of that one. She does consider the treasure hers. She be very capable of takin' what be not hers by force, and Dan be no weakling, as I mentioned, at least not in body. Ye need be very careful, for a treasure be not worth a life, no matter the size, though it took yer ancestor many a year to learn that piece of wisdom."

"We are stuck," said Owen. "We don't know where to go from here. Is there any way you can help us or give us a suggestion about where we should go from here?"

"Nary a bit, lad, not one pinch, scruple, iota, jot or tittle. Anything that I tell ye is in the strictest confidence and telling more of it would jeopardize any progress ye have made so far."

"Paddy, are you telling us that we have already made progress?" Owen asked.

"Aye mate. That I is. But I may tell ye one thing in the confidence of shipmates that have in mind the best for each other." He winked broadly and his smile grew to encompass his face. It showed his teeth that were as white as new fallen snow.

"That advice is to keep on pressin' down. Ye may get lucky yet. Meanwhile don't be looking for me the next little while, since I have business elsewhere. Mayhap I'll see you after that. Now, there's just enough time for tea and cakes."

The last thing Paddy asked us was if we remembered the poem exactly as he had repeated it to us. We had to admit that we didn't. He made us repeat it many times.

In the warm glow of the fire, our stomachs replete with sweet cakes, we began to nod off. It wasn't more than a few minutes that we slept, but when we awoke Paddy was gone, wagon, and all. Once again, we looked for the wheel ruts or a trail, but found none. Once again, he had simply disappeared into the forest without a trace, a will of the wisp, a puff of smoke, a mirage. We regrouped in the woods, to find out where to go from here. The only safe place to talk away from prying eyes or listening ears was in our secret spot. A curious sight greeted us.

Paddy was still looking after our best interest, for hanging from a nail in a tree was a scroll of sheepskin. On it he wrote a copy of the poem. Now we wouldn't have any trouble remembering it, even if our memories drew a blank. "Do you remember when Paddy told us to just keep pressing down?" asked Mike.

"Sure," I replied. "Why?"

"Don't you think that's an odd way of expressing it?"

"What do you mean?" said Owen.

"Well, you don't usually tell someone to press down. At least I have never heard anyone say it that way in America and I really don't think the Irish do either. Usually you tell them to press on, if you tell them to press at all. I wonder if Paddy was trying to tell us something in an oblique way."

"The only place that we have been down lately is the staircase that led us into the castle. Do you suppose that Paddy is telling us to return to the castle?" said Owen.

"I don't want to go down there again," Matt interjected.

"No, never again," I added.

"Even if Paddy says there is no ghost, I know what I heard. Someone or something was following us. And the screams and that laugh. That's the last place on my places-to-visit list," said Mike.

"Look, I don't want to go in there any more than any of you do, but what if that is where the treasure is hidden? We are going to lose this place if we don't find that treasure. I'm going to suggest we think about that and take a vote on the matter," said Owen.

"Okay, all those in favor of returning to the castle; raise a hand."

"Which one?" asked Matt.

"Any one," replied Owen testily.

We all raised a hand.

We were going back into the castle. We had a number of chores to attend to, prior to our next visit to that dank place of horror. Owen took the lead and assigned Matt to obtain extra batteries and some method of getting around the rats. Mike volunteered to get some snacks and sodas to sustain us. Owen was to find such things as rope and other safety equipment, since we remembered the steep climbs and drops we faced.

Since the poem had mentioned the full moon, we suspected the moonlight would help us to find the treasure. Owen found out from the paper that the full moon was tonight. It would be the last full moon before we would have to leave for home. Without the treasure, we would never see Kildare again. We had to go. It was now or never.

I don't know how I was ever able to sleep knowing that we were going into the castle again, but suddenly Matt was nudging my shoulder.

"Wake up, Taylor. It's time to go."

I opened my eyes and realized that I had slept rather soundly.

Owen and Mike were waiting for us in the library. A quick silent greeting and we made a check of the adjacent rooms. No one was there. We listened in silence for the least sound that would let us know Mrs. Greeley or Dan was about. There was nothing. It was all systems go, as I pulled the appropriate book from the shelf and the wall moved to reveal the staircase once again. We went through, careful to close the secret door behind us.

Down we went, until we reached the wooden door where Owen placed his hand in the proper place. It swung open. The first obstacle was to descend the steep staircase. Even knowing that it did end, it was still scary to contemplate the drop and the likelihood of death if we fell. But the thought of the treasure and Paddy's advice to keep pressing down pushed us on.

Dad telling us that we were going to lose the estate was the real reason that we pushed ourselves and I sure wouldn't want to lose the library. We had grown to love this place and badly wanted to keep it. We had to go on, no matter what awaited us, whether it was strange footsteps, rats, moans, demented laugher, or anything else. It was up to us to save the estate and keep it in the family.

The silence and cold penetrated as we hugged the walls of the stairs. We had roped ourselves together so that we could save each other if we fell. Except for the scuffling of our feet and our heavy breathing, there was total silence. For some reason Paddy wanted us on the lowest level, at least that's what we thought.

Have you ever noticed that when you really fear something and it is very dark, you seem to hear sounds you normally wouldn't? I don't know if I'm making sense, but I could hear the scrabbling claws of the rats, even though we were a long way from them. I shuddered with the thought that they could smell our blood and were awaiting a fresh feast. Next to whatever was in the castle, the rats were my biggest fear. Owen had assigned Matt to the rat patrol. When we asked what he had done for our defense, he just grinned in a knowing way that told us he had the situation under control. He wouldn't tell us what he had planned. I was curious as Matt often had very different solutions.

We reached the bottom of the stairs safely.

"Now what?" I asked, "Are we any closer to the treasure than before?"

"We have to get to the castle," said Owen. "I say we keep on going. I think the treasure is in the castle somewhere."

"If the *full of the moon* means midnight, we don't have a lot of time either," said Mike, "We've got to move fast."

"Why do you think the treasure is in the castle?" I asked.

"Remember the second conversation with Paddy, when we told him of Mrs. Greeley and Dan and their activities in the attic?"

"Sure," I said, not knowing where this was leading.

"He said they could look all they wanted but they would not find the treasure in the manor. He was implying that it isn't in the manor and all of their labor is for nothing. If it isn't in the manor, then where else could it be but in the castle?"

My heart was in my mouth when we approached that door again and knew what lay beyond it. We stood in indecision before it when Matt pushed it open, a wide grin on his face.

They came immediately. There were hundreds of them. The sound of their claws on the stone floor was scary. They streamed from under the walls and seemed to materialize before us, hungry and aggressive. The beams of our flashlights blinded them temporarily, but that didn't stop them. As they surrounded us, we rapidly began to edge toward the door.

"Matt, do something," I said, since it had been his job to take care of the rats. They were bolder than before, the light only holding them back for moments.

"It's time to teach these overgrown mice a lesson," said Matt, his mischievous grin illuminated by my flashlight. He reached into his pocket and pulled out a firecracker that must have been three inches long and an inch wide. It looked like a small stick of dynamite. They were the kind known as cannons.

"May I present the matches," he said as he passed them to Mike. "Please do me the honor of striking one."

Mike quickly struck the match with trembling hands. Matt stuck the tip of the long twin wick into the flame and it began to sizzle at once.

"Throw it Matt," I shouted nervously. But Matt just grinned and held it aloft between his thumb and forefinger while the wick burned quickly down to the point where it was sure to explode. Just when I thought it would blow off his fingers he lobbed it into the middle of the rat pack.

"Plug your ears," he shouted. End over end it tumbled as the wick burned to the powder.

KABLAMMMM. The firecracker exploded in the air just above the rats, sending bits of paper floating down. An instant acrid smell of gunpowder filled the air.

The noise echoing off the walls still made our ears ring, even though we tightly plugged them. When the reverberations died down there was not a rat to be seen.

"Got 'em," Matt said, looking immensely pleased, grin running from ear to ear.

We could still hear the noise echoing loudly. If whoever or whatever was chasing us before did not know of our presence, it surely knew now. But then, perhaps a loud noise would scare it away, as well. Deep down, I knew that was just hope. Still, we had passed a major hurdle and at least we knew that we could handle the rats again if we had to.

We made our way to the anteroom that was before the dungeon, ensuring that the door behind us was secure against the rats. We went to the stone benches that were against the wall to rest our legs, knees like jelly.

"Matt, why didn't you tell us what you had in mind for the rats?" asked Owen, a little annoyed at not being let in on the secret, but relieved by the result.

"Surprise, surprise," Matt answered with his infectious grin causing us all to laugh.

"Now that we don't have to worry about the rats, where do we go from here?" asked Mike. "It's only a few minutes to midnight."

"It looks like we're going to miss out on any chance to find the treasure," I added.

"Maybe," said Owen. "Let's just rest a few more moments, not that this stone bench is comfortable . . .

"Wait a minute, the lines in the poem. There's something about a stone bench isn't there?"

Since I was the keeper of the poem, I took it out and read, *"When at the place of all alone, Hie thee to the bench of stone."*

"This is a bench of stone and I can't think of any place that could be more alone. Maybe we're where we're supposed to be," said Mike.

We sat awhile, when the weirdest thing happened. Mike noticed it first and told us to shut off our flashlights. We started to question him, but he told us to be quiet. We did what he said and then turned to look at him for further instruction. He pointed to the ceiling above us. While we knew that we should have been well below ground level, we saw a thin eye of silvery light shine into the room. It was barely noticeable at first but grew brightly in intensity.

"Almost midnight," said Owen looking at his watch. "What do you think of it, Mike?"

"Let's just look for now and see where this leads. There's nothing more we can do anyway."

We watched as the light grew. The eye of light became a strong shaft that strengthened as midnight approached. The beam shone on the stone on the wall opposite us and we rushed to look at it and watched carefully as it intensified even further. It was beginning to light the entire room.

"*When from gray to silver hues the rock*," I recited from the poem excitedly.

"What?" asked Owen.

"The poem. It all makes sense. The next line mentions four eyes."

Mike ran his hand over the illuminated stone. "Look," he said, his voice gaining volume with his mounting excitement. "There are indentations here, grouped together. Four of them. Flat to the surface but rounded into the stone. I'll bet they're for the moonstones; they're about the same size. Quick, let's put them in the holes."

We all fumbled with our pouches and quickly placed them in the holes. Three stones were in place without result. Matt had not placed his yet. The light had achieved maximum intensity, soon to fade

"Come on, Matt. Put your moonstone in the hole. Quickly."

"Oh, darn," said Matt.

"What's wrong?" I asked.

"I dropped it."

"Clown," said Owen under his breath.

I heard the comment but I don't think Matt did. Not that it would have bothered him in the least.

The moon was full and if we didn't discover the treasure now, we would be back in America for good before the next full moon came. All would be lost. We scrambled to the floor and frantically searched for the moonstone.

"I've got it," said Mike, earning instant hero status. He ran to the wall and placed it. "Look," he said. The light from the combined stones grew in intensity, as if the four moonstones had garnered the light and reflected it as a greater force. That force concentrated on a stone in the floor.

Again, I read from the poem, *"Four eyes are there to light the dark; to point the way, to find the mark."*

"I think this is it," said Owen.

"Great," Matt replied. "What exactly is it?"

"Wait and see," I said.

It was fantastic. After all our adventures, here was the treasure. The beam pointed the way. We marked the stone on the floor carefully, because the light was quickly fading from full flood as the moon passed. We retrieved the moonstones and replaced them around our necks, safe in our little pouches. We took out the chisel, portable shovel, screwdriver, and hammer that Owen had procured and began to work on the stone. We scraped all around it until we had loosened and cleared the dirt between it and the adjoining stones. The grout was beginning to show. We began to appreciate how hard Dan had worked as we dug at the grout with hammer and chisel to loosen the stone. We all took several shifts until we had the grout cleared from the stone. Now came the tedious job of prying the stone loose and removing it. We had no idea of how heavy it was. We couldn't budge it. It gave us a real respect for those old time masons who had perfectly cut and perfectly placed each stone. It must have been backbreaking work. No matter how we tried, we couldn't budge the rock. We sat down to contemplate our problem.

"What about the iron bar that is used to lock the door?" asked Matt.

"Maybe we can loosen it," added Owen.

With that, we began to try to loosen the bar, but it was fitted with brackets on either side of the door. Large bolts and nuts secured these onto the door. It was fortunate for us that they were old and rusted; otherwise the task of removing them would have been impossible. As it was, it took a lot of work with hammer and chisel to get them off. This invoked a comment from Matt that he didn't realize you had to work so hard to find treasure.

Once the bar was loose, we managed to push it into the space between one stone and the next and pried as hard as we could. It moved. Our progress was slow to begin with but as we pried we stuck the portable shovel under the stone, which gave us leverage and more room to pry it further. After what seemed like an eon, we managed to tip the stone away from its resting place to reveal bare earth below. There was not enough room to dig.

"We need to pry up a few more stones or we won't be able to dig," said Mike.

The second and third stones came up much easier. We began to dig.

It was not long before the shovel hit something hard. The way it echoed told us that it was not a stone, for it had a hollow sound. That was encouraging. We all started digging with our hands. We uncovered a chest. It was very small with handles.

"Kind of small isn't it?" asked Matt, mirroring all of our disappointed thoughts.

"Yeah, and kind of light too, for something supposed to be a huge treasure," said Mike.

How could something so light and small hold a vast treasure?

The chest must have measured no more than a foot in any direction and Mike was right, it was very light. Where were all the doubloons, pieces of eight, the jewels and bars of silver and gold? We stared at it in our disappointment.

"I guess we should open it," Owen said.

He popped the clasp with a screwdriver and looked in.

"There's a parchment scroll in here," he said,

We crowded around as Owen broke the red wax seal that held the roll tight. He then carefully broke the wax seal. We trained our flashlights on the document as Owen unrolled it. It became very clear what we had in our hands. It was a treasure map.

Excitedly, we looked at the map in detail, forgetting where we were. That's when the awful sounds that we had heard before were upon us again. The sounds were growing to even greater force. The demonic screams, the evil laughter, and the shrieks filled the cavernous halls. The sounds were very near, and then they faded away only to return, as if something were searching for us.

I heard the slap of feet again, loud as if something very large was coming our way.

"Let's get out of here," I whispered, and we were soon in full flight. In my peripheral vision, I did see Owen wrap the scroll around his arm and then put his jacket on over it as he ran.

We had never been on the lower level except for passing up the stairs to the main floor. With each step everything was new, each room, every twist of corridor. I followed Mike, with Matt and Owen going in another direction. Mike and I ran until we were out of breath and had to stop to rest, having no clue as to where we were or where the others were. I was both scared of our situation and glad of Mike's company.

As we rested, we heard the footsteps echo away from us. We were safe for now.

We needed to find Matt and Owen, but we felt that it was in all our interests to be as quiet as possible to keep whatever was out there at bay. We wandered as lost souls through endless corridors, thoughts of those who had disappeared before uppermost in our minds. We loudly whispered their names to keep as quiet as possible, yet try to contact them, but we never received an answer.

I thought I had heard something and motioned to Mike to be silent. "Listen," I whispered in his ear.

"The footsteps. They're back," he whispered back. "Let's just stay here and keep quiet and maybe whatever it is won't find us."

We shook as we pushed our bodies against the wall, trying to be as invisible as possible. Trembling we waited. A huge shadowy apparition was suddenly upon us. It lumbered around a corner carrying a torch, its face a twisted image with opaque eyes. Instinctively, our self-preservation took over, our legs moving with a will of their own.

No matter how fast we ran, or how many corridors and hallways we dodged into, the evil behind us seemed to be on our heels. It was impossible to lose, but it never quite caught up with us.

A dead end did us in. It wasn't really a dead end, but a room at the end of a corridor. When we entered it, we realized there was no escape. Too late, we heard the slam of the door behind us and the ominous click of the lock. Strangely, there were bars on the inside. To our astonishment, we realized that the iron bars were a cell, and we were in it. A little light now flooded into the cell from the door.

"Ha, ha. Hugo chase strangers. Hugo hates strangers. Strangers bad," announced a booming voice as if from a very large person. But this person was small, shorter than any of us by several inches. Was this the huge apparition, which had chased us? How had he been able to make himself look so large and fearful?

"I see our friend Hugo got you, too," said Owen. In our haste we had neglected to look around but now we saw both Matt and Owen trapped in the room as well, sitting against a wall.

"Where are we?" Mike asked.

Owen shone his flashlight around the room slowly.

"Oh," said Mike, his voice sagging, "The dungeon."

I was tired, as we all were, and since there was nothing we could do about our present predicament, we sat on the floor, tired and depressed.

CHAPTER 7

Thock . . . Thock . . . Thock . . . Thock. I surfaced from sleep to see Matt throw his ever-present rubber ball against the floor. I watched it bounce against the wall, then rebound back to him, which he caught easily in one hand. With the light from the door so subdued, Matt had to keep his flashlight on to see the ball.

I was annoyed that he had awakened me. My sleep had not been comfortable and I was stiff, tired, thirsty and hungry. All of that amounted to a cranky me. I was about to tell him to stop.

"Matt," I started to say, summoning my most annoyed tone of voice, when Owen put his hand over my mouth.

"Shhhh," he said as he pointed towards the door. There at the door was Hugo, illuminated in the indirect light from Matt's flashlight. When I watched his eyes, I realized that they were following the ball. I tried to guess his age, but it was impossible. He could have been anywhere from fifteen to forty, since he had a sallow complexion, no hair and was missing all but a few of his teeth.

"He's fascinated with the ball," whispered Mike. "I wonder why?"

"Do you know you have an audience, Matt?" Owen asked in a subdued tone.

"Indeed, for about five minutes so far. I think he likes the ball," Matt answered out of the side of his mouth.

"I'm alternating between the floor and off the wall, and from the wall and off the floor, just to make it more interesting."

Matt turned to Hugo, "Do you like the ball."

Hugo grinned and nodded, "Hugo like ball."

Matt held the ball between his thumb and forefinger. "Try it," he said.

Consternation appeared on Hugo's face. You could tell he was wrestling with indecision. It was a tough call for him and we all remained silent, since we knew what rode on this decision. If Hugo accepted, it was a crack in the armor of his feelings against us. If he refused, we were in deep trouble. However, Hugo opened his hand and Matt placed the ball in it.

It was obvious that Hugo had never thrown a ball before and we were amazed that anyone his age hadn't. Hugo tried to duplicate what Matt had done. His first try was hilarious. He threw the ball so hard that it bounced off the floor, walls and ceiling and rebounded again and again. Those little rubber balls can hurt when they hit, especially when thrown with force. To see us all cowering with arms covering our heads, scrunching as small as we could to avoid this tiny object would have made anyone laugh.

Matt now became a coach.

"Do it this way Hugo. I guess I should call you Huge, 'cause it's the opposite of what you are, like they call a big guy, tiny. You can call me Matt."

Hugo smiled at Matt and we knew that Matt had made a friend. Never again would I complain about Matt and his rubber ball.

Hugo missed on his second try and Matt displayed his technique once again.

After half a dozen tries, Hugo successfully caught one. A wide grin spread across his face revealing the stubs of teeth left in his mouth. There was no doubt that the missing teeth and stubs had been from neglect. Rather than creating fearsome looks, it made me feel sorry for him.

"Huge buddy, great catch. You'll be a champ yet," Matt said.

The broad grin on Hugo's face became even greater.

Owen then spoke up. "Hugo, do know who we are?"

Hugo nodded. "Young people, strangers, bad." He started to retreat into his defensive shell and I worried that we might have lost him.

"Do you really know us? I mean our names and why we are here?"

Hugo shook his head, indicating that he didn't know.

"Then why have you locked us up?"

"Young people in castle. Bad for young people to be in castle."

"Why is it bad for us to be in the castle?" asked Mike.

"Mother say it bad. Mother always right."

"Mother, Hugo? Who is your mother?" I asked.

"Mother is mother," was his reply.

"Do you have a father?" I asked out of curiosity.

"Yes."

That was it. He had answered the question in the simplest way possible.

"Who is your father?" Owen asked.

"Father just father."

"But does he have a first name, like Hugo?"

"Father just father."

"Do you have a last name, Huge?" asked Matt.

"Don't know. What is last name, Matt? Hugo just Hugo. Hugo, huge," He smiled at his own joke. We all laughed in which he joined.

Since we were getting nowhere with this line of questioning, I decided to try a different angle. "How old are you Hugo?"

"Seventeen, I think."

"Seventeen," Owen whispered. "He looks forty."

"No," I whispered back, "Look at his face. There are no wrinkles, which you would have if you were forty. Also, the way he was fascinated with the ball, an older person wouldn't be at all interested."

"He could be mentally challenged," Mike added.

"I don't think so," stated Owen. "He understands all of our questions and answers them. If anything, he simply has no social skills. I suspect that he has never had any friends and doesn't know how to relate to people."

Owen began to question Hugo. "Where do you live, Hugo?"

"Hugo live here."

"Where? You mean here in the castle?"

Hugo nodded and went back to throwing the ball with Matt's encouragement. He may never have had a friend before, but he sure seemed to be warming up to Matt, who kept calling him Huge. I could tell he liked the nickname, since he smiled each time

Matt used it. A bond was beginning to develop between them.

In a stroke of brilliance, Mike asked, "Hugo, do your mother and father live in the castle?"

"No."

"Where so they live?"

"Hugo not know."

"That's terrible, Hugo. Children usually live with their parents. Who looks after you?" I asked.

"Why terrible?"

"Because you don't live with your parents, who are supposed to love you, care for you, protect you and teach you about life."

"Hugo not want to live with parents."

"Why not, Hugo?" I asked.

"Hugo afraid of Mother, don't like Father."

Owen again entered the conversation. "Hugo, what is going to happen to us?"

"Hugo guard for Mother."

"Would you let us go, Hugo?" Owen asked.

Hugo shook his head in denial and a look of alarm spread across his face. It was as if we had reminded him that his safety was in doing what his mother told him. He backed away from the dungeon.

"Wait, Huge," said Matt.

Hugo paused.

"We know your name but you don't know ours. Friends should know each other's names. You know mine, and this is my sister Taylor, my brother Owen and our cousin Mike. And you forgot this." Matt handed him the ball.

"This is a gift from a friend to a friend."

Hugo's eyes widened. He stared at the ball and then stared at Matt. I couldn't be sure, but I thought there were tears gathering at the corners of his eyes.

"Hugo like ball," he said thickly as he disappeared into the gloom.

"Great, now what?" said Owen to no one in particular.

If there was one face in the world that I didn't want to see, it was at the door.

"Well, well, if it isn't four lost little lambs whose parents aren't even worried that they weren't in their beds all night. But then, how could they miss yer when they're in Dublin. Lucky they have a trusty housekeeper to look after you. Oh yes, and don't expect Mary Rose to rescue you either. I told her that yer father had no further use for her services," Mrs. Greeley said with an evil chuckle. Her eyes narrowed to slits and her sour face became even more pinched and ugly. "Why are you in the castle?"

"None of your business," I shot back. "This castle belongs to our dad and we don't have to answer to you. You'll be in big trouble if you don't let us go right now."

"Well now, my snooty young girl, I don't think you are in any position to threaten anyone."

She turned to Hugo, who was peering through the grille behind her. "You said they had been digging, didn't you?"

We gasped as he answered, "Yes, Mother."

"Don't call me mother. How many times have I to tell yer that, you half-wit? Hummph," she grunted in disgust. "Well you just take me to where they was digging," She turned to us, "I'll take me leave now. See if you remember what it was that you was up to in here. Perhaps a little hunger and thirst will help your memories."

I shuddered when she had gone and Owen, thinking aloud, said, "I hate to think what she'll do when she finds the chest we dug up."

"Maybe we can deny it. After all, no one actually saw us dig it up," I suggested.

"It won't work," Mike replied. "The earth is freshly dug and it'll be obvious it was us. For sure, she'll want to know what was in the chest."

"We should have hidden it," added Matt.

"Hugo, yer did well to catch those brats, to come and get me."

"What Mother do with them?"

"Hugo, don't call me Mother. How many times do I have to tell you?"

Hugo cringed, "Yes, Mother."

"Yer incorrigible. Well, don't be takin' to them them too much. They might not be around very long, if yer know what I mean." Her nasty laugh echoed down the corridor.

"They are evil, Hugo, thinkin' that the castle belongs to them. They'll make you leave. Did they tell you that it belongs to their father?"

"Noooo," wailed Hugo, "People who make Hugo leave are mean."

"I'm glad you understand."

Hugo took her to the spot where they found the chest. She examined it, since it sat with an open lid. She picked it up and peered inside trying to ascertain what was in it. She ran her hand around the inside to see if there were any secret compartments. Instinctively, she knew that the chest was very old. Her excitement grew.

It was not only Mrs. Greeley and Hugo who appeared at the grille to confront us, but Dan as well.

"What was in the chest?" she demanded.

"Nothing," replied Owen. "It was empty when we found it."

She looked askance at Owen. "I don't believe you. Well, you can stay here until you starve to death or you can tell me and go free."

"Don't believe her, Owen," Mike said. "She'll never keep her word,"

I said, "Show us a token of your good faith by bringing us something to eat and drink and I'll tell you what we found."

"You'll tell us now," ordered Dan as he poked a shotgun through the bars causing us to hug the walls as far from the muzzle as possible.

"Take the gun away, Dan. We'll only use it if we have to. Let's play their game for now. After all, they aren't going anywhere."

It was not long before we heard the rattle of the key in the door. Dan placed the food and water in the dungeon while he held his gun on us to make sure we didn't try anything. Mrs. Greeley watched carefully.

"Now I have fulfilled my part of the bargain," she said. "It's time for you to fulfill yours. What did you find in the chest?"

"This," said Owen, as he handed the scroll over to Mrs. Greeley before we could stop him.

"No, Owen," Mike said, attempting to intercept the map. But he was too late.

Mrs. Greeley snatched the map and studied it. She looked up sharply. "Part of it is missing."

"I can't do anything about that," said Owen. "That's all we found. We think the rest of it is buried somewhere else."

"Do you know where?"

Owen shook his head in denial.

She looked at him in a way that showed she did not believe him, but seemed content to let it pass. She turned to Dan, and in a whisper that we barely overheard, said, "It's in the manor. I just know it."

Dan groaned audibly at the thought of further labors.

They turned and walked away as they talked. Owen ran to the grille and shouted after her. "What about our bargain? We had a deal."

Mrs. Greeley turned her head without breaking stride and answered. "What deal? I don't remember any deal." She laughed as she disappeared from sight. Her laughter continued until the sound died away in the halls.

"Owen, are you crazy, giving her that map?" Mike asked, the anger in his voice barely controlled.

Owen placed a finger on his lips and we fell silent until we knew that everyone was gone.

"Before you arrived, when we were caught, I figured that we would have to give up the map. I tore the part with the woods out and dirtied the edges so they looked like it happened a long time ago. I still have the part with the woods. What they have is totally useless. So far, the treasure is still ours. I didn't tell you about it because I needed you to look genuinely angry to make Mrs. Greeley believe it. Now, if we can just get out of this place . . ."

CHAPTER 8

We remained in the dungeon contemplating our fate for several hours before we heard the sound of a key in the door. I looked up, expecting to see Mrs. Greeley and Dan come to get us, but the head that peeked in belonged to Hugo.

"Hey, Huge, good buddy," said Matt giving him a light friendly tap with his fist. "What's up?"

Hugo smiled back at Matt with a smile as wide as his face. But the smile left his face suddenly. "You in danger. You come with me. Mother bad. Father bad. They want to hurt you. You not bad. You my friends. Must be as quiet as little mousie friends. Mousies only friends of Hugo until you come. You new friends. Hugo like new friends. Hugo not want them hurt. Mother say new friends take castle away from Hugo, but Hugo not believe her."

"That's right, Huge buddy. We would never do that. You're our friend."

"Thanks Hugo, we weren't looking forward to being hurt," I said.

Silently, we followed Hugo as he led us through the labyrinthine corridors of the castle with the sureness of one long accustomed to them. One could easily have been lost forever without a guide.

"Where are you taking us, Huge?"

"To manor."

"Do you know where the tunnel is that leads to the manor?" Mike asked.

"Hugo know."

"And the long staircase that leads into the manor?"

"Hugo know."

"Hugo, do you know of the door that opens to the manor?" Owen asked.

"Hugo know."

"And the one that leads into the library," Owen added.

"Hugo know."

"Huge, you are a man of many words, all two of them," Matt added. "My kind of guy."

We all laughed, even Hugo.

"Can the door at the top of the stairs to the manor be opened from the outside?" Owen asked.

Hugo nodded.

"Great. Let's go."

As we walked, Mike asked, "Hugo, does your mother know about the door into the library?"

"Mother not know."

I thought back to the frightening apparition that I had seen when we had first arrived at the manor. Could that have been Hugo?

"Hugo, have you ever been in the manor?"

"Hugo in manor. Hugo go to manor to get food. Mother forget food sometimes."

I could feel the sting of tears. Poor Hugo, he had no friends but the mice in the castle, until we came along. His mother and father cared so little for him that they treated him like an animal and sometimes forgot to feed him.

"Do you ever go outside?" I asked.

He looked horrified. "Hugo never go outside. It not safe."

"Why is it not safe?"

"Mother say castle only safe place for Hugo. Hugo hates light, sun burns Hugo's skin. Hurts Hugo's eyes. Light bad."

A look of comprehension came into Owens eyes. "I think we had better leave that one for now."

Knowing that we were free again put a spring into our step and made the climb up the stairs a lot easier. Hugo was very nimble and practically ran up the stairs, barely pausing at the landings. We had a very hard time keeping up with him. Hugo arrived at the top landing and waited for the rest of us to catch up. When we did, Hugo placed his hand on the wall and the door opened.

"How did you do that, Hugo?" Mike asked.

"Hugo place hand right here."

We pointed our flashlights at the spot and saw that there was an indentation that was barely noticeable. We had been over the wall in minute detail but we had missed it. We were all curious, but Matt asked the question. "Huge, buddy, how did you discover this?"

"Paddy show me."

Paddy. My heart skipped a beat.

"Hugo, did Paddy look like a pirate?" I asked.

"What is a pirate?"

"Did he have a big hat and a wooden leg?"

Hugo nodded again. Wow, he was one of us. He had actually seen Paddy.

"Huge, you're amazing," said Matt.

Hugo grinned widely as he opened the secret door to the library.

"Can you come with us?" I asked.

Hugo looked frightened suddenly. "Hugo not come."

"Okay, buddy. You don't have to come. We'll come back to get you later," said Matt. "Meanwhile keep practicing with that ball and show me what you can do when we get back."

"Goodbye for now, Hugo," I said as I gave him a hug. "Thanks for rescuing us. We'll see you soon. We promise." Two big tears rolled from his eyes. I had suspected it before, but now I knew. Hugo was a very sensitive and very gentle young man.

We went into the library cautiously, since we were now at the mercy of Mrs. Greeley and Dan. If they caught us there was no doubt how we would fare in their hands. One by one, we crept out of the library and into the pantry. We filled our pockets with food, since we didn't know when we would be able to eat again, and we already ate all the food we had brought with us. We went into the woods again to hide from the fearsome duo, since we needed to plan carefully.

The woods were our only safe haven. We didn't speak until we were back at our secret place and checked to make sure no one followed us. Owen had pulled the torn map remnant from his sleeve.

"As they say in the treasure business, *X* marks the spot," he said, pointing to a spot on the map marked with an 'X'.

"But the 'X' looks like it is in the woods. That can't be right. It has to be in the castle," I said.

"Maybe the map is a fake, just to throw us off," Mike added.

"If it is a fake, it sure is an old one," said Owen as he studied it carefully.

"Whereabouts in the woods is the 'X' Mike asked.

"There's a clearing by the look of it. A large one at that," said Owen. "It looks like the X is in the middle of it. We've only seen one large clearing, and that's where we met Paddy. Maybe there are others further into the woods."

Suddenly Mike got very excited. "That's it. That's it."

"That's what?" I asked.

"It all makes sense now," he said.

"What are you talking about? Stop talking in riddles. What makes sense?" Owen asked.

"The last line of the poem. You know, where it says: *The end is found right at the start.* Don't you see?"

"I don't have a clue what you are talking about. Explain please."

"Where did we first find out about the treasure?"

"From Paddy."

"That's true, but that's not what I meant. Where we were when we first learned about it?"

"Where we met Paddy."

You could almost see the light turn on in Owen's mind.

"In the clearing where we first met Paddy. The large clearing."

"Exactly. The treasure is located where we first learned about it. *The end is found right at the start.*"

"I think you may be on to something. Let's give it a try."

"Okay," said Owen as we arrived at the clearing where we had met Paddy. "We need to take stock. If we are going to find the treasure, we have to think this thing through. We don't want to do half a job and have to leave the treasure dug up and exposed while we find something to handle it with. Now we are assuming that the treasure is both large and buried. What equipment will we need to get at it?"

"A shovel," Matt volunteered.

"Right. We have the portable one but we'll likely need something a lot larger, with a long handle to pry the dirt loose. The treasure could be buried very deep. Maybe we'll even need more than one. A pick or mattock wouldn't be a bad idea, either. What else do we need?"

"How about some rope and some pulleys?" Matt added. "The treasure will likely be heavy and we'll have to drag it out of a pit that could be very deep."

"That's right," Mike said. "And if the treasure is really heavy, which is likely, with gold and silver and all, we'll need a way to get it back to the manor."

"That's a good thought," said Owen. "The paths in the woods are narrow. Any ideas?"

Yes, I thought, the paths do seem narrow. Narrow, narrow. The word went through my mind repeating itself over and over again. In a sudden leap, it jumped to barrow. Then I envisioned a wheel. "How about a wheel barrow?"

"Brilliant," said Owen.

"Okay, let's assign tasks. We'll need to buy a few things. Let's pool our money and see how much we have."

By the time we had counted our money, we had forty pounds between us. To tell the truth, I never got used to the Irish money system. Prices were in pounds or guineas. A pound is twenty shillings and a guinea is twenty-one shillings. Does that make any sense? Just to confuse matters more, a shilling is also called a bob. A pence is a penny. There were half pennies called ha'pennies, and there were a tuppence or two penny coin. It would have been bad enough to figure out if they left it at that. They didn't. There were farthings and half farthings. I haven't any clue what those are worth. Just in case you thought you might figure out the system, there are also crowns and half-crowns. Good heavens.

Now just try to figure out what they mean when you try to buy something and you ask how much it is. They might tell you four guineas, six shillings, tuppence, or maybe a crown, a couple of bob and two farthings. I just held out my hand and let them take what they would. You have to be born into this money system to understand it. I shouldn't say that, because somehow Matt had figured his way through the arcane system and was able to translate it to our money, but then he had a mind for math. It was a good thing, since Matt and I went to Mick's to get the rope and shovels. Owen went with Mike to look for extra shovels, pick, or mattock, and pulleys at the manor.

Owen and Mike found a block and tackle. I never knew what a block and tackle was. The blocks are a set of three pulleys and act as a focal point for lifting. The more ropes that connect the blocks to other blocks, the easier it is to haul a heavy load upwards. This way, the power of a person is multiplied many times.

Owen and Mike went back to the manor, since there was a garden shed, where Dan spent most of his time. We thought they might be able to find what they needed in there. A few hundred feet separated the shed from the manor and cottage. It stood in the open with a large bush to one side. Bent low, the two ran to the back of the shed and remained hidden from the view of the manor. Mike peered around the corner, saw no one, and went in. They took the block and tackle, which they placed in a wheelbarrow and, checking to see if anyone was watching, left the shed for the woods.

We met again in the woods. Mission accomplished. There had been some money left over, so we thought it our duty to provide sustenance of a non-healthy variety. We bought delicious candy, potato chips, and all sorts of fat-filled snacks for energy. For thirst, there were lots of sodas, or pops, as the Irish call them. Not one of us felt guilty about it. We had earned it by dint of our intelligence in solving the treasure puzzle.

We arrived at the clearing. I thought that it would be a simple matter of digging at the spot marked with an X and we would live happily ever after. Some fairy tale that was! It appears that nothing in life comes easy.

Owen brought up the first problem. "As near as I can figure, this map is over four hundred years old. I think that there's every reason to believe that things have changed. Enough time has elapsed that the trees will have entirely changed. Most would be dead. Some may still be around, but they would be huge now. New ones will have grown as well."

"Oh, great," Mike said, "That's all we need."

Owen continued, "The writing on the map is faded and very hard to read, but I think it reads

"Wak ye fiftiee paces doo est frum the midrif of the ril wer it tuches opon yon medoe."

"Gee, they really knew how to spell in those days," said Mike, "Whatever does it mean?"

"I think it means to take fifty paces from the middle of the stream in a due east direction."

"Why didn't they just say it like that?"

"This is early English. At that time, England was still a very parochial society and the language was still developing. England was the result of a mixture of races and their languages over the centuries. They had their own tongue and all contributed to the emerging English language. That's why English is such an adaptable language and why it is so difficult to learn, and a lot of the time doesn't make sense."

"That's more information than I needed, Owen," Mike said. "How big were people back then, I mean the ones who paced it?"

"This could take forever," Matt added.

"Good point," said Owen, "We need to make some assumptions. As an educated guess, I would say Paddy was about the size of whoever paced it off to begin with. You're about his size, Mike. Why don't you pace it off?"

"Giant steps or small steps?" Mike asked with a gleam in his eye.

"How about regular steps?" said Owen with an edge of sarcasm in his voice.

"I think I know where it is leading, but I want to be certain before we start to dig," said Mike.

Mike paced it due east, according to the position of the sun that rises in the east. He halted before he took the final step, since he was about to step into the fire pit where we had sat with Paddy the first time we had met him.

"Do you think it's under there?" Owen asked.

"I can't think of a better place to hide a treasure," Mike said.

We started to dig. First, we cleared the ashes from the pit and rolled the stones that surrounded it well clear of the work area. Mike and Owen took the first shift.

"How far down do you think it is?" Matt asked.

"How high is the sky?" asked Mike.

"How deep is the sea?" said Owen.

"Maybe to China," I chimed in.

"What is the sound of one hand clapping?" Owen added.

"If a tree falls in the forest . . ."

"Alright, alright," said Matt laughing, "Stupid question."

We took turns, since the job was turning into a big one, a lot bigger than we had bargained for. The deeper we dug, the wider we had to make the hole. It also got harder and harder to toss the earth out, as we got deeper. I suppose we all imagined it would be only a few feet below the surface. I was beginning to wonder if we had made a mistake on the location, as we alternated turns with the shovels. Our heads disappeared below the surface, the deeper we dug. We had to stop to dig a ramp, since we were now so deep that we couldn't throw dirt out by shovel. We used the wheelbarrow to extract the excess dirt, but it soon needed two of us to push and one to pull as the slope became steeper and steeper. We then attached the block and tackle to a tree and began to use it to help us pull the wheelbarrow up for emptying. It was totally exhausting.

Matt asked the question that was on all our minds. "How far down are we going to dig before we admit that there is nothing here?"

It wasn't a popular question, but we needed to face it. We determined that we would dig another hour and then reassess the situation.

"That is, if China doesn't come first," Matt said.

It wasn't another five minutes before we heard the sound of a shovel striking something hollow that was definitely not dirt or stone. Mike was on shift at that time and his shovel was the one that struck. He dug and felt around the object, eagerly assisted by the rest of us.

"Sure does look interesting," said Owen as he jumped into the pit and brushed dirt from the top, revealing the carved wood and what was apparently leather that had mostly rotted away. Was this it? Had we found the treasure?

We continued to dig around it with greatly renewed energy, but we couldn't budge it. We couldn't open it either, since our ancestor had wrapped it with old chains, and locked them together with a thick old padlock, which had rusted shut. That meant we couldn't open it without hauling it out of the hole. As near as we could estimate, the trunk was eight feet long, four feet wide and five feet high. It was a monster. Now this was a treasure.

"Gold sure weighs a lot," said Mike.

"And a lot of gold weighs a lot," Owen added grinning.

"We need to set up a tripod," said Matt.

"There is some deadfall in the woods. Maybe we can use some of it," Mike said.

"It'll be strong enough if it is fairly recent. Let's go get what we need," Matt added.

We managed to bring three thick and strong-looking pieces, but it was hard slogging. The idea of digging for buried treasure seems easier than the reality. We secured one end of each piece of wood by placing it into the ground six inches so that it wouldn't slip when pressure was put on it.

We knew the trunk weighed a lot but didn't know how much. Matt had to shinny up one of the logs with rope to tie the top of the tripod together. The tripod was almost ten feet high. He tied one end of the block to the top and let the ropes dangle from it. Next, we secured the chest to the rope by tying it around either end and then making a sling to which we could attach the dangling rope with one of the blocks that had a hook. Mike pulled on the rope until it was taut. Owen began to pull with him. I watched them both strain.

"Taylor. Matt. Give us a hand."

"Okay," said Matt, "A hand you shall have." He began to clap his hands again.

"Get over here, you clown," demanded Owen, not the least bit amused.

Upwards we hauled until the trunk was suspended above the hole.

"Now, what?" Mike asked as we looked at the trunk dangling there without any way to land it.

"We have to shovel dirt underneath it and raise it a little at a time," Owen suggested.

We left Mike and Owen to hold the trunk in place and Matt and I shoveled dirt under it. It was almost as hard as digging the original hole, but now that we had the treasure, the work went faster. It took us another hour, but we finally had the trunk out of the ground, with a nicely filled hole under it.

We were about to try to open the top when we heard the sound of two hands clapping.

"Well done. I want to thank you for findin' the treasure for us."

There was Mrs. Greeley, with an evilly happy look on her face. I could have smacked her face to wipe that know-it-all grin away.

"How did you know what we were doing?" asked Owen looking about as crest-fallen as I have ever seen anyone.

"Sure weren't hard. Who did you think you were foolin' with that half map you gave me. Take me for daft do you? The half you gave me showed that the treasure wasn't to be found in the manor or the castle. I waited until you fools came to the shed to get the tools you needed. I saw you, but you didn't see me.

"That halfwit who calls me his mother had his role to play, too. I told the simpleton that I was going make sure you were out of the way. You should have seen how agitated he became. He really thought you were his friends, isn't that funny?" she laughed. "He really thought he was foolin' me when he set you free. He didn't know that I was using him. Bygorra, imagine that moron thinking he could outwit me."

I was about to correct her on that notion when Owen began to speak. He looked at her and said. "What makes you think we'll let you have the treasure?" He and Mike took a step towards her. Mrs. Greeley shrank before them.

"Stay where ye are," shouted Dan with his booming voice. Out of the woods he came, over to Mrs. Greeley. His shotgun leveled at us. The four of us froze.

"Now it looks like we'll need a hand with that trunk and you'll help if you value your hides."

We worked under the threat of Dan's shotgun, while Mrs. Greeley disappeared and returned with a horse and cart.

"So ye thought a wheelbarrow would carry out all that treasure, did ye?" She laughed again. "Best open the trunk so we can see what we finally have, Dan. Need to know if there really is a treasure."

Dan used a crowbar to snap the bonds that held the top securely in place. He raised the lid and all was silent as the mound of gold coins crowded the top and spilled onto the ground. We nearly died as Mrs. Greeley whooped in delight and danced a short jig with Dan as they celebrated their newfound wealth.

They tied us to a tree after they forced us to help load the treasure, but other than that, we were unharmed. As they climbed onto the cart, we heard Mrs. Greeley say, "The government of Ireland need know nothing of this. They'll just take half of it in taxes. If we quickly leave Erin, it'll be all ours."

We watched as the cart with the trunk full of treasure, our only chance to save the estate, moved away with the laughter of Mrs. Greeley diminishing as it disappeared.

"We should call the police," I said, feeling a deep anger at the outrage that had been perpetrated upon us.

"Sure," said Owen. "And tell them what? That we discovered a treasure, and it was stolen from us. I'm sure they'd believe us. Wouldn't you believe a bunch of kids whose ages range from fifteen to seventeen? Wouldn't you order a general alert for two adults who had stolen a treasure chest?"

Tears of rage ran down my cheeks at the unfairness of it all.

CHAPTER 9

"It's so unfair. There goes our estate, castle, manor, and our Paddy."

I was feeling sorry for my parents, my brothers, my cousin, and myself when I heard a familiar voice.

"And where is it that ye are assumin' Paddy has gone?" said a wonderfully familiar voice.

"Paddy," we shouted in unison.

Paddy came to me.

"Oh, Paddy. We found the treasure and then we lost it. You were right, Mrs. Greeley did not deserve it, but she got it in the end. Now we won't be able to keep the estate and worse, we won't ever see you again." That thought sent a huge tear rolling down my cheek.

"Here now, me sweetheart, calm yourself," he said as he moved his finger up my cheek to wipe away the tear. "This tear is special and I place it in your pocket for ye to remember me by." He made the motion of placing the tear in my pocket. It was touching.

"I'll never forget you, Paddy. Not as long as I live."

"Ooch, lass. Ye put me in mind of one I knew many a year ago. Like you, she was a comely one. Remember always that ye have the blood of the O'Neills runnin' in yer veins and that is a mighty proud thing. Paddy knows many things and one of those is that ye will have a life filled with love. I want ye always to remember that love is all the treasure ye'll ever need. It makes earthly riches meaningless. That advice comes from many a year of experience."

"Paddy, can you help us to get free?" asked Owen.

"Well, in a manner o' speakin . . ."

"Oh no, not that again," Matt said, "Why can't you just untie us?"

"I am sworn by oath. I cannot help in any direct way. But there is one thing I can do. I can hint. Ye'll have to draw the conclusions on yer own. There are rules o' the tinker trade, with which I must abide. I can't untie ye. But I can say the knife in Matt's back pocket might be helpful. Still, that might be pushin' the edge and considered interferin'."

Owen fished the knife from Matt's pocket and was able to saw the ropes that bound Matt's hands. Matt freed the rest of us.

"Let's get Greeley and Dan," said Owen, ready to pursue.

"I would not do that if I were you," said Paddy, "Besides, they're long gone."

"But we found the treasure. It rightfully belongs to us. Mrs. Greeley and Dan took it from us without any right. It's gone forever."

"That all depends now, doesn't it? Does the treasure rightfully belong to ye or not? Paddy has learned much during his lengthy sojourn on this mortal coil. The first lesson is that treasure be a transitory thing. Would ye no agree with me that in the beginning it belonged to the Spanish? From them it was seized as spoils. Mayhap afore that, did it belong to the Indians, by their enforced labor in the mines? Who knows how countless were the lives lost in the pursuit of riches for Spain? Perhaps yer ancestor has to answer for his privateering ways. Aside from all of that, there is the matter of the shotgun that Dan wields. Now, I will tell yer with great feelin' that there is no earthly treasure worth losin' yer life for. On this earth the greatest possessions are love and life."

"But Paddy. Mrs. Greeley and Dan have the treasure. Is that fair?" I said, interrupting the silence.

"What is fair in this earthly existence? They have only the treasure of which they are deservin'."

"But they have the treasure. Are they deserving of the treasure? You said before that they were not deserving of it. I still think it is unfair," I said rather hotly.

"Lovely missy, they have the treasure that rightfully belongs to them. That is a fact we cannot dispute. Long gone are they by now, with no thought other than to be as far away from this place as they can, until they are so far away that they can count the treasure in peace."

"But they still have the treasure."

"Ah lass, ye seem to have a mind that has only one thought. Now I am tryin' to tell ye something, and ye have no thought for listening."

If I needed proof that Paddy was human, I had it. I detected impatience coupled with a tinge of testiness. Were ghosts testy? I didn't think so.

"Okay Paddy, I know when I am being lectured and I don't enjoy being lectured. What can you tell me 'in a manner o' speakin'"

"The missy has not lost her sense of humor, I see. 'Tis all well and gud, as they said in the old days. As I mentioned durin' one of our earlier meetin's, there was a final verse that I couldn't remember at the time. It left me memory as sure as eight bits make a piece of eight. Ye have to understand that privateers were very clever and none was cleverer than that ancestor of yers, that first Earl."

Paddy seemed to preen as if the praise was meant for him, and he paused for a moment as if waiting for nods of approval. None came, since all of us were more than a little put off by Paddy's attitude.

"'tis by the most fortunate of circumstances that I am here to encourage yer forward search. I am in memory of the last stanza of the riddle. It goes like this.

> *When ye delve in a pirates brew*
> *Whatever's lost is found anew*
> *Believe ye not what finds the eyes*
> *The top can be a fair disguise.*

"Now, I'll be takin' me leave of yer. I wish ye God Speed and the best that ever befell mortal man. Better shipmates a privateer never had."

We watched Paddy walk away. I wondered if we would ever see him again. His wishing us *God Speed* seemed like a final farewell. None of us quite knew when he disappeared from sight. We were watching him and he just faded gradually from sight, like a mist under a rising sun. He was there and then he was gone.

"How does he do that?" asked Matt.

"The treasure is still there," said Owen, "The line, *whatever's lost is found anew.* It's still there."

"But we saw Dan and Mrs. Greeley take it away. How can it still be there?" Mike asked.

"I don't know, but we have to dig again."

Matt groaned, "China again."

We went back to the site. Our tools were still there, so we once again took shifts. The loosened earth was easier to dig so the progress was fast until we hit untouched earth below where we had dug to before. Our shovels began to hit objects with hollow sounds and we pulled up four chests, smaller than the first one, but still large and very heavy and cumulatively a lot larger than the first. Knowing that we had no time to lose, since Mrs. Greeley and Dan might yet return, we worked as we had never worked before. Sweat poured from our brows from the mighty effort, but this time we were going to keep what we found. With Owen standing guard at the dig site, we moved the chests one at a time into the manor and stowed them safely in one of the bedrooms upstairs. Only when we had it all in one place did we breathe easier.

CHAPTER 10

Mom and Dad returned from Dublin the next day in a downcast mood. The negotiations with the government had not gone well. They told us that we would be leaving soon, and that we should consider this trip just a nice holiday. The estate would revert to the government at the end of the month, since the duties would remain unpaid.

"The secession duties are cast in stone," Dad said, shaking his head sadly.

"Tell me Dad, if you could find a way to keep it, would you?" asked Owen.

"Owen, that's just dreaming, there's no way we can keep it. We just can't afford it. End of story. But, for the record, I'd keep the estate. I've grown to love it and it feels more like home than home does."

"Okay, we have a surprise for you and Mom. It's upstairs in one of the bedrooms, but we want you to close your eyes when we get outside the door. We'll take you there, and until we tell you, don't open them."

"This feels silly, but okay let's see your surprise." said Dad

We led them to the bedroom and they shut their eyes until they were completely in the room. We had opened all the chests and mounded the gold and silver bullion, doubloons, and jewels on the bed and floor. It was a vast treasure, which had broken the legs of the bed, but we really weren't worried about that.

"Open your eyes."

Dad just stood there, his jaw dropped in awe. "What? . . . how? . . . good heavens!"

"Oh my," was Moms reply, "Oh my, oh my, oh my."

"Where did all this come from?" Dad asked, still stunned by the enormity of it all.

"Rainbows, Dad. We were chasing rainbows," Owen answered. "It's the legend of Padraic O'Neill, our ancestor. We found it with the help of a gh . . ."

"Leprechaun," Mike added quickly, "And he showed us the end of the rainbow."

We explained as much as we could. We did not refer to Paddy, since we felt that they wouldn't understand. Adults block that sort of thing out of their minds. Both Mom and Dad were saddened to hear of Hugo and his loveless existence.

It turned out to be a treasure almost beyond reckoning. The Irish government took half and I am sure they were as well pleased as good queen Bess was in her day. As a family, we all agreed that half of our share would be set aside for charitable works. We split the remaining portion. Half went for the ongoing maintenance and improvement of the estate, and to make sure it remained in the family for a few generations yet. The balance, we split in equal shares between Mom, Dad, Hugo, and us kids.

Speaking of Hugo, we brought in specialists to examine him, after we calmed him down and promised not to bring him into daylight. Within a matter of weeks, his extreme light aversion abated and he was able to be out in the daylight. His skin began to take on some color and that made him look normal. The latest advances in dentistry gained him gleaming white new teeth that made his smile attractive. Psychiatrists were consulted. They felt his progress was such that he would be a functioning member of society in a few years. They also found out that he had one of the highest IQ's on record. Hugo was a genius.

We spent a lot of time with him, since he was living with us for a while. And though Mom and

Dad constantly admonished Matt for calling him Huge, Matt never stopped. I think they finally realized that there was a special bond between them, and Hugo loved the nickname Huge. He started calling Matt, *Rug*, since he claimed Matt was too big to be a mat.

Mrs. Greeley and Dan disappeared. They never did contact Hugo again. He was better off for it, since he was so unloved by them. He wouldn't be alone anymore, as he had us.

I should tell you that when I put my hand into my pocket (the one Paddy put my tear into) I felt something round and pulled it out. It was a teardrop pearl. I have no idea how he did that, but it hangs from my neck on a chain. I will treasure it all of my days. And the moonstone will always be a special treasure for me. I made it into a ring in a silver setting. I wear it to this day, as a constant reminder of that amazing person.

Mary Rose is now our full-time housekeeper and her husband is the general manager of the estate. They have taken a special shine to Hugo, who now lives in the manor when he is not in his special school where he boards. Both give him great hugs and they are starting adoption procedures. They have such a depth of love in them.

That summer was the best summer of our lives. We learned some very important lessons from our

Irish sojourn. First and foremost is that money is not the root of all evil. A great many good things can come from money. It is the love of money that is the root of evil. I believe that the lust for the treasure was what turned Mrs. Greeley and Dan into such twisted people.

Also, I learned that it is the striving for a goal that is the sweetness of the adventure, not necessarily the attainment of it. That is almost anticlimactic. I often think back on our great adventure and wish that we were still looking for the treasure, terror and all.

I know that you are wondering what made those scary noises in the castle. Well, I'm not going to tell you, but if you ever come to Kildare, I'll let you stay in the castle for the scariest night of your life. Hugo will see to that.

When we left Kildare that summer for *The Americas*, I saw Paddy in the airport. No one else saw him, even though he was in his pirate's garb. He looked at me with his big blue eyes, looked left and right, and placed his finger on his lips commanding me into silence. He swept his big hat off his head and swished it to one side as he bowed in a courtly fashion. He then blew me a kiss and disappeared into the crowd.